For more than forty years,
Yearling has been the leading name
in classic and award-winning literature
for young readers.

Yearling books feature children's
favorite authors and characters,
providing dynamic stories of adventure,
humor, history, mystery, and fantasy.

Trust Yearling paperbacks to entertain,
inspire, and promote the love of reading
in all children.

OTHER YEARLING BOOKS YOU WILL ENJOY

SAMMY KEYES AND THE SEARCH FOR SNAKE EYES
Wendelin Van Draanen

SAMMY KEYES AND THE ART OF DECEPTION
Wendelin Van Draanen

PIRATE ISLAND ADVENTURE, *Peggy Parish*

THE GHOSTS OF COUGAR ISLAND, *Peggy Parish*

THE MYSTERY OF HERMIT DAN, *Peggy Parish*

SPYHOLE SECRETS, *Zilpha Keatley Snyder*

THE UNSEEN, *Zilpha Keatley Snyder*

PURE DEAD BRILLIANT, *Debi Gliori*

THE HAUNTING, *Joan Lowery Nixon*

MIDWINTER NIGHTINGALE, *Joan Aiken*

The WICKED WICKED LADIES in the HAUNTED HOUSE

MARY CHASE

Illustrated by Peter Sís

A YEARLING BOOK

Published by Yearling, an imprint of Random House Children's Books
a division of Random House, Inc., New York

Visit us on the Web! www.randomhouse.com/kids

Educators and librarians, for a variety of teaching tools, visit us at
www.randomhouse.com/teachers

ISBN: 0-440-41956-5

Reprinted by arrangement with Alfred A. Knopf Books for Young Readers

Printed in the United States of America

August 2005

10 9 8 7 6 5 4 3 2

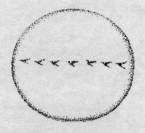

FOR SHEILA CHASE
—M.C.

CONTENTS

THE OLD MESSERMAN PLACE

Maureen Swanson was known among the other children in her neighborhood as a hard slapper, a shouter, a loud laugher, a liar, a trickster, and a stay-after-schooler.

Whenever they saw her coming they cried out, "Here comes Old Stinky," and ran away.

Sometimes she would pretend she hadn't seen them. She was a good pretender. If she was pretending she was a queen or a movie star or Maureen Messerman, she would not notice. At other times she would chase them, slap the one she caught, then run and hide until the trouble died down.

Her mother often said to her father, "How I wish Maureen could be a little lady: sweet, kind, and nice to everyone."

He frowned. "She better learn to mind first. She better stop hanging around that Old Messerman Place."

The Old Messerman Place, which took up half a city block, was walled in, boarded up, deserted. You couldn't see inside because the brick walls were too high, and the spruce trees growing just inside the walls grew so tall and so close together that even when you threw your head back and looked up, all you could see were four chimneys like four legs on a giant's table turned upside down.

In the middle of the wall that faced the boulevard hung a pair of high, wide iron gates across a bricked driveway where once carriages pulled by horses had gone rolling into the grounds. You couldn't see where they had rolled or where they had stopped because just inside the gates tall wooden boards were nailed together and a sign read: *Private Property. Keep Out. Trespassers Prosecuted.*

Some people insisted the Old Messerman Place was haunted, that at night they often saw lights flickering through the trees and in the daytime they heard a tap-tapping kind of sound like someone pounding with a hammer in there. Occasionally the neighbors called the police, who came down the boulevard with sirens screaming, unlocked the gates, pried open the boards, and looked around.

A row of pigeons, huddled close together on the roof, would watch with beady eyes as the officers tramped through the garden with flashlights, up and down the stairs, in and out of the rooms in the big empty mansion, never finding anything or anyone. For a few days after these visits the garden would be dark at night and silent in the daytime. Then the lights would flicker again and the tap-tapping sound was heard as before.

Boys were always trying to climb over the high walls. One would stand on the shoulders of another and reach high up, straining and straining, only to jump down panting.

"Can't make her. She's too high."

Maureen Swanson never tried to climb in by straining and reaching high. What she did was talk to herself as she stood by the gates, her fingers holding the iron posts.

"I'm Maureen Messerman. That house is *my* house."

One day, two weeks after her ninth birthday, she came home late from school. She had been kept by the teacher to write twenty times on the blackboard: *I must not start fights on the schoolground.*

She was in a bad humor as she picked up the hose lying on the lawn in the Swansons' backyard, turned on the water full force, and sent the dry leaves scurrying across the grass, fastening them up against the side of the house. Then she waved the hose up and down and across the house itself, across the windows of the Moodys' house next door, and then across Mrs. Moody's clean laundry drying on three lines.

Mrs. Moody ran out of her house. "Stop that," she screamed. "Stop that—you brat."

"*You* brat," Maureen shouted loudly, and then she waved the hose up and down and across Mrs. Moody herself.

"I'll fix you." Mrs. Moody was running across the lawn. Maureen dropped the hose, ran out of the back gate and down the alley. She could hear doors slamming, voices raised, and her mother's voice calling, wailing, "Maureen. Maureen, you come back here."

She ran up the street and was flying past the Old Messerman Place when her eyes lit on the boards behind the gates. One board hung open, nailed carelessly after the last visit of the police. She pushed against it and it fell back. She wriggled through the iron palings of the gate, got inside, pushed back the board, and stood against it listening as the feet ran by on the walk outside and the voice called, "Maureen! Maureen! Come back here."

She looked around. She was in a large garden, overgrown with high grass and weeds. The tall spruce trees grew close together on all sides like protecting, green-needled walls. Across the garden stood a house almost as big as the post office with many windows and balconies, and a wide stone porch with no roof, shaped like a stage and encircled by a low stone balustrade.

Three broad steps led down into the garden.

Bushes and grass were growing between the posts of this balustrade, between the bricks on the floor of the porch, and at the wide brown wooden door, as though everything in the garden was trying to grow its way up and into that house. There were no curtains at the windows. Maureen counted four little balconies of stone and iron on the house, four pairs of glass doors behind them. The two windows above each of the balconies looked like eyes watching her.

She waded now, knee deep through the grass and weeds, to a little pool set in stone like a swimming pool, but it wasn't. An iron boy with an iron fish in his hands looked at her with vacant iron eyes as he held the fish high above the pool, as though just about to throw it into the water below, which was covered with thick, slimy green moss. Paint was peeling off his arms. Maureen broke off a weed and poked at the moss in the water. She stopped as she heard a tap-tapping sound. A woodpecker, she decided. She smiled and looked for him in the spruce trees but the blue sky got in her eyes. White snowy clouds were moving lazily across the blue. They looked like one big snowman rolling after three little snowmen. She sat down in the grass and watched them happily. Then she lay down and looked up. Wasn't it wonderful in here!

She sat up quickly when she heard the tapping sound again. Listen! Yes, it was coming—not from the trees—but from there!

A little house, a summerhouse, made of wooden strips, criss-crossed, stood away back at the other end of the garden. She waded through the grass, hitting at it with the long tough weed in her hand. The tap-tapping got louder. She peered through the open door of the summerhouse. The tapping stopped. The woodpecker had seen her. He *was* in the summerhouse.

At first she couldn't see anything. Then her eyes, getting used to the dim light, found an old porch swing, a broken lawn mower, a hose coiled in one corner, the rubber peeling off like a snake shedding its skin. Near that was a tall iron birdbath, cup side against the floor. In another corner, on a small pile of old rotting canvas, sat another garden ornament—a little old man with a long white beard and a tall cap, sitting cross-legged on the canvas, holding a shoe in one hand, a hammer in the other.

She had seen garden figures like him many times, sitting beside flower beds or rock gardens. They were called something funny like "leppercons." They usually wore green painted suits and tall green hats. This one was different, she decided, because his hat was brown and it wasn't painted. It looked like it was knitted, like the kind of cap a schoolboy might lose on a winter afternoon. And he wasn't wearing a green suit but something that looked like an old undershirt, and his pants could have been made of a piece of the canvas on which he was sitting. There was something else different about him, too. One cheek was puffed out like a squirrel with nuts or a child with the mumps on one side.

The light now seemed to pour in brighter through the latticework strips of the summerhouse, but she could see no woodpecker. Turning to leave, she stopped still as she heard a sound like "pish."

She saw the little man spit a nail out of his mouth onto the canvas. Then he put down the hammer, picked up the nail, held it against the sole of the shoe, and pounded tap-tap-tap.

She heard a small thin voice saying, "And *who* are you?"

Her mouth fell open. He was *real*!

Now there are two kinds of people in the world, who behave in two different ways when something unexpected happens. Most people take a step backward. A few step forward with a clenched fist. Maureen was one of these. She stepped forward and shouted, "Who are *you*?"

The little man now raised his head and looked at her. His eyes were bright blue in his brown, wrinkled face. His eyebrows were gray and bushy. He did not blink as he studied her closely.

"Glory be—if it ain't Maureen Messerman!"

She didn't know her mouth had fallen open. Had she said that out loud as she stood by the iron gates?

"Close yer mouth," he told her as he got to his feet. "Ye'll catch flies." When he stood up he was the size of a five-year-old child.

"How do you know?" she asked him, so surprised.

"I know lots of flies."

"How do you know about—oh, you know—what you just said just now?"

"What did I say? Sure I say lots."

She was getting cross. She stepped closer to him and made her voice low. "That name—Maureen Messerman?"

"Oh, that." He sat down on the canvas cross-legged and picked up the shoe and the hammer. "A bird told me."

"A bird did *not*. What bird?"

"Oh, a fair-sized bird, bigger than a sparrow, not as big as an owl." There was a frown on his forehead as he lowered his voice. "Sure now you better be gettin' out of here and not comin' back again—ever."

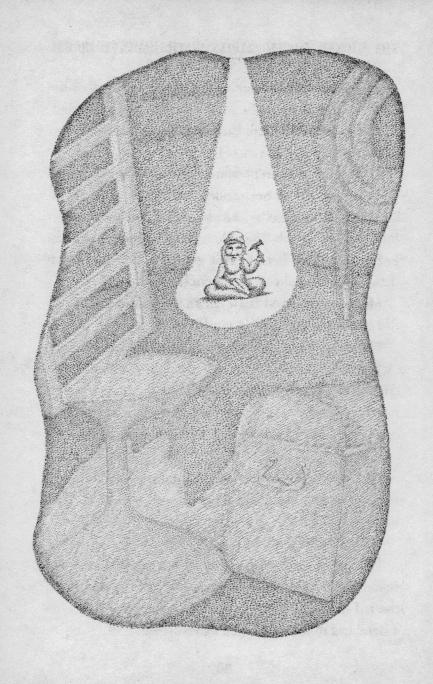

Maureen didn't get out. She came closer to him. "That bird. He's a liar."

The little man shook his head. "Not he—she."

"Then she's a liar."

To her surprise he nodded and the long gray beard made a swishing sound against the canvas.

"And she's no lady." He pounded the nail deeper into the sole of the shoe. "You can't fool me on a lady. I seen one once here in this garden—with her seven little daughters, sittin' on a bench out there."

Maureen followed his eyes as they looked out into the garden near the little pool.

"There's no bench there now," she told him.

"There's no lady neither and no seven little daughters." The little man looked sad. He had forgotten her. He was looking at the spot where the bench had once been. His blue eyes now looked like seawater.

"What did the lady do?"

"If I was to tell you that, we'd be here all day. She lived in there," and he nodded toward the house. "She was scrumptious."

"What's scrumptious?"

He took a long time about answering that one. He made out like he was dusting the sole of the shoe with the tip of his beard.

She began again. "What's scrump—"

10

"It's what she was." He sighed.

"You're silly," she told him. "You're just crazy, silly."

He nodded again. "Maybe," he agreed, "but not so silly that I think my name's Maureen Messerman."

"Stop saying that," she shouted. "Don't you say that again. My name's not Messerman. I only say that sometimes. That's—pretend."

He wiggled his little brown forefinger back and forth at her. "Ah now, pretend—that's tricky. Be careful. First the whisper. Then the big wind. What happens is . . ."

He didn't finish it. He heard something and he held one finger under one ear and listened.

"Here they come," he whispered to her. "The fun's over now sure. Off with you if ye know what's good for yez and *don't* ever come back."

She heard a loud flapping of wings as a flock of gray pigeons flew over the tops of the spruce trees, across the garden, and came to rest on the roof of the house. Pigeons! Only pigeons!

The little man was gone. Where? She ran around in back of the summerhouse. No one there. Only a carpet of brown pine needles. Had she dreamed him? No. Looking in the summerhouse again, she saw a smooth place on the canvas where he had been sitting. The shoe and the hammer lay to one side.

"Hey," she called out, "where are you?"

Nobody answered. The pigeons on the roof were sitting huddled close together, looking at her with beady eyes.

She walked around the garden and pushed back the needled branches of every tree, looking underneath. Where could he be? A little wind blew against the screen in front of the big brown door of the house. It hung by one hinge and whined in the wind. The house! He was in the house!

She ran up the steps and held her hands on either side of her head as she put her nose against the glass of the window and peered inside.

It was so big in there—and so dark. Dimly, she could see a great empty room with a high ceiling, a black marble fireplace with a tall mirror above it. The mirror was cracked, with zigzag cracks like a glass map. From the high ceiling, from a hole with broken plaster around it, a dusty chandelier hung by one wire, as though someone had tried to swing on it and pulled it loose.

As she pushed on the front door, she heard a creak-creak sound and waited. Then she pushed harder and the door swung open. She was in a big dusty hall with a wide staircase before her, going up, up, up. The stairs stopped at a landing with a tall dusty window.

Maureen walked slowly into the room with the chandelier hanging by one wire. Everything was covered with dust. The wall was stained with water spots. In some places the plaster underneath was showing. The room looked like someone who has waited for years in all kinds of weather for someone else who never came.

Where was the little man? She heard a noise and ran into the hall.

What was that? It sounded like a rustle of something moving somewhere. He was upstairs, maybe. She slowly climbed the stairs, stopped at the broad landing, spit on one finger, rubbed a clean spot on the dusty glass, and looked down into the garden. There was the pool, the summerhouse, the tall trees, and the weeds—all quiet, dreaming. She couldn't see the little man anywhere out there. She heard a rustle sound again, like somebody moving somewhere. It seemed to come from the hall at the top of the rest of the stairs, which turned here and climbed up higher.

"Hey," she called. Her voice sounded small and whispery. "You up there?"

The sound of her own voice scared her and she almost turned to hurry back down when out of the corner of her eye she saw a flash of color—something red—no—yellow.

She looked and saw standing there a lady with a long yellow dress, a fan held in one hand before her face. Maureen stared and the lady seemed to stare back at her. It was a picture. She ran up the stairs. Pictures all over— on both sides of a big wide hall—pictures of elegant ladies, all wearing beautiful long silk party gowns. Gosh!

Maureen stopped by the first one in the yellow dress. One arm was behind her back and the white fan was held against her face just under her dark eyes. Her hair was black and her skin was so white. On a brass plate fastened into the frame at the bottom was the name: MAVIS.

Maureen looked at it for a long time.

"You're too skinny," she told her, and went to the next one. She was in green silk, striped with blue satin. Her hair was red. Two little curls hung from either side of her face.

She held in one hand a white teacup with a gold rim. The brass plate beneath her said: CLEO. One arm was behind her back.

"Cleo," Maureen said out loud, "that's silly."

Constance was the next one. Her cheeks were pink and her hair was brown. A black cape fell from her shoulders to the floor. It was lined with red over a long red dress. In one hand she held a white rose. Her other hand and arm were behind her back.

Next was Lucrece. What a funny name! When Maureen said that one aloud, she said, "Lucreaky."

Her dress was purple with tiny silver stars. She was holding nothing. The fingers of one hand touched the stones of a necklace at her throat. The other arm was behind her back. Maureen did not like her much.

"Fooey to you," she said, and moved on.

The next one wore a long white cloak. One small hand, gloved in red, held the cloak together. You couldn't see the other arm. It was inside the cloak. Her hair was silvery blond and her eyes black. She was Maude.

"You stink," Maureen told her.

The next one was the most beautiful. Her gown was silver and gold, with a gold sash. Her hair was gold, too. One bare arm hung down by her side. The other was behind her back. This was Sylvia.

"You're the best," Maureen told her.

At the last one she said "ugh" and made a face. This was the seventh one. She was Ingrid and she was so ugly. Her nose was crooked and her mouth big. Her eyes were small and green and her hair was pale yellow. But the dress was the prettiest yet. It was all silvery and cloudy and billowing and soft green. She wore a green glove on the hand that held the side of her skirt. The other arm, like all the rest of them, was behind her back—almost.

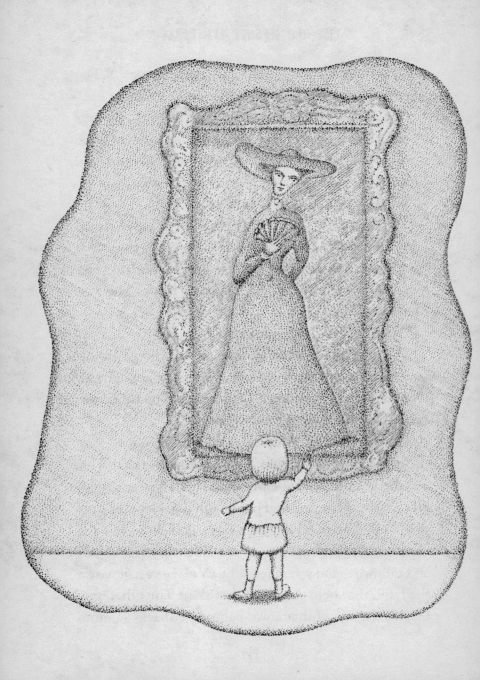

It looked like the painter had painted her just as she was about to put her arm behind her back.

What a funny bracelet! Hanging from Ingrid's wrist, on a little gold chain, were pigeon feathers!

Maureen looked at her the longest. She didn't know why. As she turned to go back down the stairs, she stopped and wondered. The pictures!

The one holding the teacup, for instance. A minute ago she had held it up high. Now the teacup was close to her mouth. Maureen was sure the lady with the fan had been holding it under her eyes. Now it was held against her chin, and her mouth was slightly open, showing little white teeth between a pair of red lips. The one in purple, too. Her fingers had been touching the necklace. Now they were at a buckle at her waist.

Moving pictures!

She waited quite a while before she gently touched Mavis's skirt with her finger to feel the paint—to make sure.

She didn't step forward then. She ran down the stairs as fast as she could, kicking up the dust as she flew out of the front door, down the crumbling steps into the garden.

She had touched—silk!

THE FACE IN THE WATER

Maureen was running so fast across the garden she didn't see anyone until she heard a boy's voice saying hatefully, "Hey, Stinky, your mother wants you and so does my mother."

This was Delbert Moody, the boy next door, standing in the weeds by the pool. With him were Junior Boggs, who lived across the street, and his young sister, Beverly, who was called Baby. *They* had come into the garden through the opening in the boards. The boys were looking around curiously, inside the Old Messerman Place for the first time.

Baby Boggs pointed a finger at Maureen. "You better not be in here, Maureen Swanson. They'll put you in jail."

She had been so frightened she was glad to see even them, her worst enemies. She wasn't frightened now. So she said, "They will *not* put me in jail. I play here lots."

How they laughed.

"You're a liar," said Delbert, "a big fat liar."

"I am not," she shouted. Then, looking nervously back at the house, she stepped closer to them, lowered her voice, and said, "And I saw something you never did see—a real leppercon."

"A real—what?" Junior was puzzled.

"That's crazy. There's no such thing." Delbert's voice was jeering and sneering.

Junior Boggs held up one finger. "Hey, listen," he whispered, "what's that?"

From someplace in the garden came again the sound of tap-tap-tapping.

"That's him," Maureen whispered.

'That's a woodpecker," said Delbert.

Maureen waded through the weeds toward the summerhouse.

"In here." She crooked her finger. "I'll show *you*."

The children looked all around the summerhouse, at the peeling hose, the broken lawn mower, the birdbath with the cup side down, and the pile of rotting canvas in the corner. Then they laughed. "Old Stinky, she's always lying." And they ran to play by the pool with the iron boy.

She followed them. "He was here a minute ago. Sitting in there, pounding a nail in his shoe."

"Get lost," cried Junior as he jumped on the back of

the iron boy and beat his feet against the sides, yelling, "giddyap."

"I did see him." Maureen's face was red. "And in there in the house there's magic pictures. They move when you're not looking."

"Magic pictures?" Baby Boggs was impressed. "Where?"

"Come on, I'll show you," she said, and she ran up the steps of the porch.

The children stood in the big dusty hallway and looked around. Everything was still.

"It's scary," whispered Baby Boggs. "Let's go home."

Suddenly Maureen wanted to say, "Yes, let's go home."

But Delbert Moody demanded, "You chicken? So, Stinky, where's the magic pictures?"

Junior Boggs pointed to the dining room across the hall. "There's pictures," he said as he ran into a room Maureen hadn't seen.

It was paneled in brown wood, once beautiful, perhaps, now warped and split with time. Above the wood, halfway up the walls, was a wall covering of woven tapestry with scenes of castles, rivers, bridges, and girls sitting with lambs.

"Where's the magic?" Delbert slapped the walls and thick clouds of dust flew out.

"They're upstairs," Maureen answered slowly.

"Show us, you creepy creep." Delbert was coughing from the dust.

She was glad when Junior called from the kitchen, "Hey, look at this crazy kitchen."

There was an old-fashioned black stove, with six round iron lids and a chimney pipe going up to and through the ceiling. The sink was tin, now blackened with age, and there was a ridged wooden drainboard. Through a big hole in the rotting linoleum on the floor you could see to the cellar below. Things were piled high down there, wooden boxes with old musty, mildewed dresses and hats spilling out, funny trunks with strips of tin and brass on top and leather handles on the sides.

They heard a slam-bang noise and everybody jumped.

A black cat with four white feet sprang up through the hole in the floor, jumped on the drainboard of the sink, and looked at them through yellow eyes. He was crouching like a tiger. Baby Boggs moved closer to her brother, Junior.

"I'll shoot him dead," Delbert bragged, "when I get my tiger gun next Christmas."

"I'll shoot *you*," Maureen shouted, "with *my* tiger gun." She liked cats and dogs.

Suddenly the cat's ears flattened against his head as though he were listening to something, somewhere in the house. His hair stood up on the back of his neck. He sprang off the drainboard, leaped over the boxes piled high on the back porch, went through a hole in the screen, and disappeared.

They all stood very still, and then Delbert motioned to them to follow him and they tiptoed into the hallway and looked around.

"Anybody home?" called Delbert bravely, when he was sure nobody was. "Anybody home?"

"He's a crazy cat," Delbert told the others. "He is real mixed up. So watch me."

He ran up the stairs, got astride the dusty banister, and slid down, slipping off the newel post. Streaks of dust now soiled his white corduroy pants.

They all slid down the banister, laughing and yelling. Then Delbert raced all the way upstairs, and they heard him calling, "Come on up. I can see our school from here."

In the upstairs hallway, Maureen and Baby Boggs stopped and stared at the framed pictures of the ladies.

Delbert had thrown open one of the bedroom doors and was now standing outside on one of the little balconies.

"That's our school." He was pointing to a flagpole in the distance, the flag waving against the deep blue of a range of mountains.

"Look. I can see our house, too."

The bedroom, Maureen noticed walking in, was papered in a design of faded pink roses, so old-fashioned and yet, she thought, somehow so sweet. There was a small fireplace with a marble mantel.

They all stood now and looked up at the tall, gilt-framed pictures of the ladies in the hall.

"Maude," Delbert read the nameplate. "She's Maude."

Maude's eyes looked back at him steadily.

Maureen whispered to them, "Shh! Come here."

When they were down the hall, away from the pictures, she made her voice so low they had to lean over to hear her. "They're magic. When you're not lookin'—they move."

"Move?" Junior's eyes were wide.

"Let's see if Maude moved."

Maude hadn't moved. She was looking straight ahead, her dark eyes motionless, her dress still as air.

"Touch," Maureen urged. "Go on—touch her dress. I dare you."

Delbert put a grimy hand on the dress.

"So what?" he now scoffed. "What's magic?"

Maureen saw his fingers touch a painted surface. She must have *thought* she touched silk. She knew they hated her more than ever, but she felt better.

"Maude stinks," she told them, "and look at these other ones, too."

"This one's Mavis." Delbert was examining the next one. "What's that she's got in her hand?"

"A fan, stupid." Maureen laughed. "Lookit me." She spread her fingers apart like a fan and stood like Mavis, trying to look silly. Not afraid now, she made a face at Mavis and said, "She's too skinny."

"Don't," said Baby Boggs, for some reason stepping back.

"I will, too," Maureen answered. "She's only a picture. There's one more, and is *she* ugly—ugh."

In the seventh frame, there was no picture!

"Ingrid's gone." And she was so surprised. "There were seven—I counted."

"You can't count," said Delbert, who was now racing down the back stairs at the other end of the big hall. This was not wide like the front staircase, but only a narrow winding hall with strips of dirty brown wallpaper hanging down like the branches of a weeping willow tree.

Maureen was telling herself, "I did count seven—didn't I?" when she heard Delbert cry out and saw him pick up something he'd found on a step.

It was a bracelet kind of thing—a circlet of a gold chain with little loops, and from each loop was hanging—a pigeon feather!

24

Delbert wouldn't let them hold it, but only feel it.

"Finders keepers," he warned, putting it into his pants pocket.

In the kitchen again, they poured water into the tin sink, water which Delbert found in a can outside the back porch.

The drain in the sink didn't work. The water lay like water in a dishpan. A few black beetle-looking bugs welled up from the drain and flapped frantically in the water.

"Bugs." Baby Boggs made a face. "I hate bugs."

"Boggs hates bugs," Maureen said, and laughed loudly.

"That's not funny." Junior Boggs pushed her. "You're a creep."

"You're a creep," she shouted, and gave him a hard slap.

"I'll show you." He charged at her but she ran out of the front door and into the garden.

She could hear them calling after her. "Go home, Stinky. Magic—fooey," and things like that.

She was wading through the weeds toward the gate, feeling cross and unhappy, when she stopped and listened. There it was again, that tap-tapping. She turned back to the summerhouse.

She looked behind a tree, but he wasn't there. She saw Delbert and Junior and Baby come out of the

house, cross the garden, and go out the gate. It was then she saw something fall out of Delbert's pocket as he reached for his Scout scarf to tie around his neck.

Running to it, bending over it, she saw it was the bracelet he had found on the stairs—the gold chain with the pigeon feathers. She put it into her pocket and went back to sit by the little pool and wait for the little man. There wasn't a sound in the garden. She poked the slurpy masses of moss apart with a long dry weed. Now she got on her knees and looked over into the black water below. She could see her own face in it, like in a mirror. She tickled the surface of the water to make her face go rippling into pieces. As the water stilled again, she was lifting the weed to poke it when she saw in the water, next to her head—another head—a face looking down—a face with yellow hair, a big mouth, and a crooked nose—Ingrid!

She ran and she didn't look back or stop running until she turned into the back gate of her own yard. It took her a long time to get her breath.

The pictures were magic!

They moved—out of the frames!

She would never, never go back to the Old Messerman Place again! That is what she thought. The wicked pigeon ladies had other thoughts—wicked thoughts!

* *

The little old man was watching as the door of the house was flung open and six ladies in elegant long silk gowns, holding lighted candles, came out on the porch and peered across the garden, as though searching for someone. They moved gracefully from one end of the porch to the other, passing each other like dancers on a stage.

It was Mavis who called out in a silvery voice, "Leaper! Leaper! Are you there?"

"Here." He stood up and brushed the twigs off his old canvas pants. She led the way over to him and lowered her candle to look into his face. He made a low bow. The ladies waited for him to stand up straight again. He didn't.

After a minute, it was Cleo who knocked on the back of his bowed neck with her fist. "Stand up straight, Leaper. Never do a bow—by half."

He stood up. "Excuse me, ladies. I got sidetracked watching this ant fellow down in the grass, forgetting, God forgive me, the glory of yer presence and the shimmer of yer shine."

The six ladies, surrounding him in the dark garden in their old-fashioned long silk dresses, all smiled proudly.

"Thank you, Leaper," Maude said, and inclined her

head. "Well-dressed you are not, style you do not have—but good manners—with your betters—ah, yes. Please nail up the board in the fence so those detestable children cannot return."

"Children?" he asked. "Was there children—where?"

"One vile child especially," said Maude. "The one who calls herself Messerman. She looked at me and said, 'You stink.'"

"She said what?"

Maude began again. "She said . . ."

Here Constance laid a gentle hand on Maude's wrist. "Sister, please, do not use such vulgar language."

Lucrece, or Lucreaky, as Maureen had said it, was pouting. "She looked at me and said—'fooey.'"

"She called me skinny," said Mavis.

"She said I was the best," smiled Sylvia.

Maude frowned. "Nevertheless she is a vile child and you will please nail up the board so she cannot return."

"Not yet," said a voice. The sisters whirled around. Who was this coming toward them, wearing a wide black hat with a yellow plume, once curling surely, now drooping down sadly? Her skirt was long and the jacket of the suit came down almost to her knees.

"Ingrid," cried the sisters, horrified, in one voice. "Street clothes, after six in the evening! How unfashionable!"

Ingrid's face was terrible to behold as she lifted her arm and showed a bare left wrist. "My bracelet fell off somehow. I saw that vile child pick it up and put it in her pocket."

The sisters moaned in anguish. "Dearest, dearest Ingrid." And they fluttered around her, cooing like pigeons. She was past sympathy.

"Less gush," she said as she pushed them away, "and more action. I'll need your help to retrieve it. Follow her by air and I'll follow you on foot."

When she said "on foot," she spat it out as the Leaper spat nails. She yelped in pain as she was pinched by the boards and the iron posts, but she did manage to squeeze herself through and walked rapidly up the street. In a minute the Leaper watched six pigeons come up from the chimneys and fly across the garden.

The pigeon ladies were fancy dressers, high flyers, smooth talkers, and hard haters. He hoped the child could lose them. How good a loser was she? And that, he knew, was the whole thing, in a nutshell.

THE LADIES IN THE PICTURES

When Waldo P. Messerman, the railroad millionaire, built his mansion and planted his garden and brought his bride, Augusta, there to live, it was so long ago there was neither an automobile on the streets nor an airplane in the sky. Horses went clop-clopping down the dirt roads, pulling grocery wagons, coal wagons, and ice wagons, too, for the refrigerator had not been invented and there was nothing electric in houses.

When you looked into windows at night, through lace curtains, you could see a family sitting around a table which held a kerosene lamp or sitting in a room with gas lamps on the walls. These gas lamps burned with a blue kind of flame and made a little sputtering sound. The very poor and the very rich used candlelight; the poor always, because candles were cheap, the rich sometimes, because the flames of a dozen candles on the dinner tables flickered so beautifully across polished wood or linen and reflected tiny lights from jeweled necklaces, bracelets, and earrings.

There was no central heating. The rich warmed their houses with firewood laid by servants in fireplaces built in every room, the not-so-rich with small potbellied stoves, and the very poor with only a stove in the kitchen, around which the families would sit on cold winter nights and around which the children would dress themselves, shivering, on cold winter mornings. Sometimes, if there were no little potbellied stoves in the bedrooms, the children would carry heated bricks, wrapped in flannel, into the icy bedrooms, lay them between the icy sheets on the bed, and hold their feet against them to keep warm until they went to sleep.

There were no telephones, television sets, radios, movies, or stereos. But there were sleds for the children in winter, horse-drawn sleighs for the grown people. Most girls and boys took piano lessons or violin lessons. After dinner, the one who had "practiced" and had a gold star on his music lesson would play for the family. The family sometimes grouped together by the piano, singing.

Waldo Messerman, while his house was being built, traveled all over Europe to buy chairs with gilt legs and satin seats, hand-carved chests and beds and tables, a chandelier and a grand piano for his fine house. He came back home, married his bride, smiled at her as he handed her out of the carriage drawn by four horses, and said, "My dear, this house is your wedding present."

The bride and bridegroom stood on the steps as the vans of furniture lumbered and teetered and swayed back and forth as they were pulled through the gates by horses. They watched as the movers carried the fine furniture inside and set it carefully down on the polished floors. Then, arm in arm, they walked inside, and so they did not see the big wooden trunk carried in the back door and up the back steps to the rooms on the third floor where the maids and the cook would live.

This trunk belonged to a little Irish parlormaid who would answer the door, serve the meals, and dust the furniture in the big rooms. And what *she* didn't know was that a real leprechaun had gone to sleep in her trunk as it stood open in a garden in Ireland.

He thought it was a woodbox, and covered himself with a blanket he found in it. So you can imagine his surprise when he woke up and found himself being tossed back and forth in the hold of a ship on the high seas. And you can imagine *her* surprise when she was unpacking her blankets and dresses and a little old man jumped out of her trunk, leaped to the windowsill, and sat himself cross-legged there, looking around curiously.

"Shame on yez," said Nora, in a scolding tone

because she had seen many like him hiding in the woods near her old home in Ireland but never one this close to her.

"Crossin' the high seas on *my* ticket. Go on back where ye belong. Do ye want to cause me to lose my place here in my first job in the U.S.A.?"

No, he didn't want to do that, and he could have gone back, because leprechauns know all kinds of magic from a "bag of tricks" which some keep in a little brown leather sack around their wrinkled old necks.

But just then he looked down into the garden. He saw the young bride sitting on the stone rim of the pool beside the iron boy. How beautiful she was! Beauty always softened his bright little blue eyes. But there was beauty back home, too. It was what she said and the way she said it as she spoke now to her bridegroom standing beside her.

"We are fortunate," she told him, "but we must never forget those less fortunate. As long as we live here we must feed the hungry, clothe the naked, visit the sick, and comfort the sorrowing."

Waldo Messerman was rich, but his bride was richer.

The leprechaun decided he would stay. So he leaped out of the window, hid himself behind a chimney until dark, and then leaped off the house, into a tree, onto the roof of the summerhouse and then he slithered inside, crouched down, and laid himself low. He was not only a leprechaun, he was a slitherer, a croucher-downer, and a lier-lower—and, incidentally, a gent.

The Irish parlormaid would hurry out to the summerhouse at night and leave a glass of milk or a piece of pie or a bit of meat on the floor for him.

"Why do you leave that food in the summerhouse, Nora?" asked Waldo Messerman one day.

"Oh, sure now, I leave it for the birds," she told him, crossing her fingers. He laughed and lit his pipe.

Hiding himself behind garden tools, the leprechaun, whom Nora named "the Leaper," would watch the bride as she strolled around the garden, picking flowers, trailing her fingers in the pond.

He would crouch lower whenever she said, "Somehow, I always feel that when I walk in my garden, someone is watching me."

"Birds, ma'am," Nora would tell her nervously. "There's birds all over the place." And there were. Pigeons flocked to the broad roof and the chimneys of the Messerman house.

As time went on, the bride no longer walked alone. A little girl walked with her, then another and another and another, until the day came when there were seven pretty little girls running around the garden in white dresses with pink sashes, their braids and curls bobbing up and down as they played tag or hide-and-seek.

It was a lovely sight to watch, so no wonder the leprechaun smiled as he watched them. So one day when Ingrid, the eldest, ran into the summerhouse, the leprechaun did not hide. He was very fond of children and had often talked to them in the woods back home. He found their conversation interesting—more interesting than grownup talk.

"How are yez?" he asked Ingrid, his eyes sparkling.

"Ugh," she told him. "Scat!" And she stamped her foot as she might have done to a mangy cat. Then she picked up a hoe to hit him.

This didn't frighten the leprechaun. He knew many tricks. He knew, for instance, how to make himself disappear—*whish*—like that. So the next thing Ingrid knew she was hitting at the floor of the summerhouse—at nothing. So she threw down the hoe and ran back to play.

She was not like her mother, he knew then, even though her hair was the same silky texture and her cheeks the same apple-blossom pink. Ah, well, he would wait and make friends with one of the others, and maybe all of the others. In the meantime, he enjoyed watching the mother and her children in the garden in the daytime and at the dining table at night, where glossy gold-rimmed plates were set around a shining table with candles. Nora stood by Waldo Messerman's side as he carved the roast and spooned up the potatoes and vegetables onto the plates. Then she carried a plate first to the mother and then to the seven little girls.

He was watching them through the window one night when he heard Augusta Messerman say to them, "And tomorrow we shall drive into the poor section of town and take baskets of food to the hungry."

He saw a frown cross seven white foreheads and a curl twist seven pairs of lips.

Only Ingrid spoke. "What shall we wear?" she asked, and listened with interest to her mother's answer.

"You shall wear your green coats, your black boots, your green bonnets, your gray knitted gloves."

"Our gray gloves?" This was Mavis. "No muffs?"

"You will each be carrying a wicker basket," her mother reminded them, and they all said, "Oh, that."

As time went on and the Messerman girls grew taller, they grew more fashionable and more clothes-conscious.

On the day for visiting the sick or comforting the sorrowing or feeding the hungry, Mavis would often say, "Excuse me today. Today I have a fitting at my dressmaker."

Or Cleo would pout, "I must go to the hairdresser."

And then Mrs. Messerman would climb into the

carriage with only Nora to help her carry the baskets or the cheerful word, while the sisters stayed in their rooms, combing their hair, or went shopping in the stores, matching foulard and serge, challis and ribbons.

Mr. and Mrs. Messerman would tell each other, "The girls will grow out of it." But as time went on, they grew more and more into "it." "It" meant coldness, selfishness, small-heartedness.

One day their father spoke to them sternly. "You will go with your mother this afternoon on her charitable calls. You will not go shopping. So dress yourselves accordingly."

Seven sullen faces stood on the porch waiting for the carriage to roll up to the steps from the carriage house behind the mansion.

A flock of pigeons flew over the garden.

"Look at them," said Maude to her sisters. "They can fly where they wish and do what they will. I envy them."

"Fortunate birds," Cleo said. "They do not have to visit the dull and dirty poor."

"How wonderful it would be—to be as free as the pigeons." Ingrid smiled as she watched them. "How I wish I were one of them now."

"Me too," echoed each sister from the bottom of her small stony heart.

When the carriage rolled around to the steps in

front of the house, pulled by the trotting horses, the porch was empty. A wind was blowing against the leaves of the bushes by the steps, making a dry, whispering little noise.

"Girls," called Mrs. Messerman from inside the carriage, "come on. I'm waiting."

She sent the footman inside to find them.

Nora came out behind him. "Excuse me, ma'am, but the young ladies came outside here to wait for yez."

She and the footman looked carefully all over the garden, in all the rooms of the house, even the attic, in the carriage house, the summerhouse, and the cellar.

"They went shopping on foot," Mrs. Messerman decided sadly. "We'll go on as I planned."

When the carriage rolled back through the iron gates, it was dark and cold. The candles were lit in the dining room, and the glossy white plates with the gold rims were set between the silver on the polished dining-room table. The light from the candles flickered on the tapestry on the walls, woven with pictures of castles and bridges and shepherdesses in long full skirts sitting beside sheep.

No, the young ladies hadn't come home. They must have finished shopping. The stores were now closed. Visiting friends? Since there were no telephones, Mr. Messerman didn't take off his greatcoat at all. He got back into his carriage and went searching. No one had seen them.

Had they gone on a trip suddenly? No, their clothes were all hanging in the closets of their rooms. They had been kidnapped! The police were notified. Descriptions of the seven daughters were sent all over the country. The weeks went by.

There were many idle, foolish reports. Some people swore they had seen seven girls boarding a ship for South America; some swore they were now dancers in a cabaret in New Orleans. Every report was investigated. None were true. The Messerman parents never saw their girls again. Sadly, Nora and the cook packed away their clothes in trunks and put the trunks in the cellar. Mr. and Mrs. Messerman grew old within a week. He took to using a cane whenever he walked. She fell ill and stayed in bed.

The people who came on foot through the iron gates! There were so many it looked like a party in the big house, except that these people were shabby and looked around so shyly as they were ushered into the big room. Many of them carried packages wrapped in newspapers; small jars of jelly or soup; some brought flowers.

"Is there anything we can do for *her?*"

"Your prayers," Nora would tell them in a whisper, "for her and her daughters."

Nora always felt like saying "cruel daughters," but she didn't. Of the leprechaun in the summerhouse she demanded, "Is this something from your bag of tricks?" She studied his wrinkled old neck. "And by the way, where is your bag of tricks?"

"It's hid safe—from everyone but meself."

"Then it's the devil's own work," she insisted.

"It's bad, bad," he agreed, "but who knows? Some good may come of it—sometime—somehow."

"Divil a bit," she answered as she hurried back into the house. Now only a light shone here and there, where before every window had blazed.

Mr. and Mrs. Messerman soon came to be known as "Old Mr. and Mrs. Messerman." One day she died. Old Mr. Messerman died shortly after and then people came and moved out the furniture. Nora wouldn't let them take the trunks of clothing.

"Who knows?" she told Lizzie, the cook. "Those girls might come back sometime, and how they did love their clothes!"

She went away herself, riding out of the gates in a wagon with her wooden trunk beside her. She had looked for the Leaper to say goodbye, but she couldn't find him. He was hiding. He never cared for goodbyes. But he watched her leave, crouched down beneath a bush.

The gates were locked then and boarded up. Before long he discovered somebody had stolen his bag of tricks, which he had hidden in a deep hole behind the canvas in the summerhouse. He sat still for three days and three nights on the top of the canvas, thinking about this. Who had stolen it? It was dangerous in the wrong hands. Anything could happen now. He suspected Nora. And he knew if she were the culprit she could get out beyond her depth. Then she would have to come back and ask his advice. This thought made him smile and then sing the words of a song he had often heard them sing around the piano in the house: "Wait 'Til the Sun Shines, Nellie."

Now, as he sang it, he changed the word Nellie to Nora and made the song go this way:

Wait 'til the trouble, Nora, foolin' with my bag of tricks, you'll find yerself, dear Nora, in some fix.

He lived on vegetables from the kitchen garden; fresh vegetables in the summer, dried vegetables in the winter, which he kept in a hole in the ground.

The house crumbled, the garden grew to weeds, but Nora never came back again.

One November evening, after many years had passed, there was a thick fog crawling like smoke through the streets. The cars were moving slowly, honking insistently, down the wide boulevard which now ran past the Old Messerman Place. The mist hung like gray silvery draperies around the tops of the spruce trees. The Leaper was in the summerhouse, reclining on the pile of canvas, watching it, enjoying it. It was a change. Seven pigeons flew over the trees and came to light on the roof. When he looked again, he couldn't see them and he told himself they were huddled behind one of the chimneys.

Soon he sat up straight and then leaped off the canvas as he saw lights in the house, flickering in the hallway, on the second floor, on the third floor, and in the cellar. Then, to his amazement, the front door creaked open and a lady in a long coat, holding a lighted candle in one hand, moved out onto the porch. She held the candle high as she peered out across the misty garden. Now the door opened again and six other ladies, in long, old-fashioned coats, carrying candles, came and stood beside her. The coats, he could see, were dusty and split with age in some places, but the ladies wore them proudly as they came down the garden steps, picking their way through the high weeds and grass. Their candles shone in the water of the little pool now brim full of rainwater. It was the Messerman girls come home! They hadn't aged a day or changed at all.

"Glory be," he cried out in astonishment. "Is it yer-selves come home, after all this time?"

Mavis moved her candle close to his face. Sylvia and Cleo took tight hold of his arms.

"What is it?" asked Constance. "Some kind of animal?"

"Yes." That was Ingrid who laughed. "It's the lep-rechaun. I remember him. He lived in the summer-house. Nora used to feed him."

"Where is Nora?" Mavis asked him. "And where are Mama and Papa?"

"Everybody's gone long ago," he answered them as the two sisters still held him tight and the others stood about him in a half-circle, looking down at him, their candles held lower now to look into his face. He shook his head.

"Shame on yez," he said, and frowned at them. "They looked and they waited and then—whoosh, they were gone. First herself and then him. Where did yez go?"

"Where does the wind go?" Ingrid said, and smiled, and the sisters smiled, too.

"We were gone only one afternoon," said Maude. "They really might have waited."

"However," Ingrid reminded them, "we do have the place to ourselves now."

"No more dull visits to the dreary dirty poor." Maude sighed happily. All the others sighed happily, too, except Sylvia. She lifted the skirt of her long coat, worn and hanging in strips.

"What a pity! I always adored this coat," she moaned.

The leprechaun was shocked. Not one word of grief about the parents whose hearts they had broken. Only the sad sigh about the clothes.

"I'll thank yez," he said as he tried to wriggle himself free again, "to return my bag of tricks."

"Oh, that," Ingrid laughed merrily. "We threw that away after we learned every trick you had in it. Hold him, sisters, and let me get a stick or a hoe to finish off the nasty little creature."

But they couldn't hold him. He slipped out of their grasp, leaped onto the roof of the summerhouse, and looked down on the seven sisters, getting soaked in the softly falling drizzle. But, then, so was he.

Ingrid tried to hit him with the long-handled hoe, saying, "Take this."

"Take what?" He'd grin and leap away.

She couldn't touch him. He laughed.

So she threw away the hoe and smiled up at him with a false smile, mysterious and deadly. Her sisters fixed their faces in the same false smiles and regarded him fondly.

"Dear leprechaun." Ingrid's voice was soft. "Let us be friends." To the others he heard her muttering, "I'll get him—later."

They couldn't beat him at this game. So he removed his damp brown knitted cap from his shiny bald head and let the rain spill onto it as he smiled at them.

"Sure'n it's fine to see yez back," he told them, "in yer glory and yer grandeur." To himself he muttered, "But I'd sooner have snakes."

They didn't hear this. They curtsied low in the wet weeds as seven heads bowed in the rain.

"Thank you kindly, Leaper; we shall be so happy here together."

Then they filed across the grass, up the porch steps, and into the dark house which snuffed out the candles.

He wondered, in a few minutes, what kind of a black crawling thing it was coming up out of the chimney and letting itself flap down to the roof. It was a pigeon. He looked closer, knowing it would be impossible for an ordinary pigeon to fly up that narrow chimney, once having fallen into it. But then he saw another and another until now there were seven, huddled close together, looking down at *him*.

He shuddered.

The Messerman girls were now weird creatures,

able to turn themselves at will into birds of the air. They had always been coldhearted, picky, flighty. Now they were demons sure. Nobody ever stands still. But this—this—

"Yer a disgrace," he grumbled in his beard, "to all decent pigeons."

THE STRANG LADY
ON THE FRONT PORCH

When she saw the lights on in the Swansons' kitchen, Maureen felt relieved. This meant dinner was not over yet. How big was the trouble about her at home? She had her own way of finding out.

Softly she opened the screen door of the back porch, tiptoed to the kitchen door, opened it only just so far, and pushed one arm through. She always did this. If there was a loud angry outcry from inside at the sight of her arm, she turned and ran and hid in the neighborhood, waiting and watching from behind something while her father and mother, big brother and sister went searching, calling her.

"Maureen! Maureen!"

When it was safe, she would run into the house, take off her clothes, climb into bed, and pretend to be asleep.

When they came back and found her, Mrs. Swanson would say, "Look at her. She's sound asleep. She's worn out. I'll talk to her in the morning."

If the trouble was small, her mother would see the

49

sweatered arm thrust through the kitchen door and sigh wearily. "I see you, Maureen. Come on in and get washed for dinner."

She said this tonight, and so Maureen was walking across the kitchen floor when her dad, reading the sports page in the breakfast nook, said, "Where have you been?"

"Oh—nowhere," she answered.

He would not drop the subject. "Why did you turn the hose on Mrs. Moody?"

"She called me a brat," Maureen shouted.

"Mrs. Moody called you a brat?" Mrs. Swanson's voice was shocked and indignant. "She didn't tell me *that*."

Henry, fourteen, and Diane, sixteen, now came into the kitchen. The television was blaring in the living room.

Henry pointed an accusing finger at his younger sister. "Maureen turned the hose on her first," he told his parents. "We saw her, didn't we, Diane?"

Diane nodded. "You must do something about her, Mother."

"You shut up." And Maureen raised her hand and ran toward her. Mr. Swanson caught her by the arm.

"You *are* a brat," said Henry.

"Don't quarrel, children." Mrs. Swanson was carrying

the plates into the dining room. "Someday you will be thousands of miles from each other."

"Goody, goody," Maureen shouted, and ran from the room.

That night, at dinner, Mrs. Swanson remarked, "You're not eating, Maureen."

How she laughed and laughed. "Not eating Maureen! How can I eat—myself?"

Nobody else laughed. It was best to ignore her.

Then she asked suddenly, "Did anybody ever live in the Old Messerman Place?"

Mr. and Mrs. Swanson exchanged glances.

"That's no place for you to play," Mr. Swanson said. He held up the fingers of one hand and knocked down each finger with the forefinger of his other hand as he listed the reasons why not.

"First, you could fall in that pond and get drowned or you could fall off one of the stone balconies and maybe break a leg or you could get splinters in your hand from one of those rotten old boards and maybe come down with an infection, or you could break one of those windows and get us hauled into court by the heirs."

"By the hairs?" Maureen was indignant. "Nobody better haul me no place by my hair."

"Quiet," warned Mrs. Swanson. "Daddy has the floor."

Maureen thought this was a silly thing to say. Daddy had an ear of corn and he was eating it.

"Besides all that," Diane said, "everybody says it's haunted."

Mrs. Swanson was studying Maureen. "You didn't go in there when you ran away, did you?"

"Me?" she laughed. "I did *not*."

"That's good." Mr. Swanson reached for the salt. "Because you'd be punished if you had. I've told you never to go in there."

Mrs. Swanson was serving the dessert when the doorbell rang. Mr. Swanson opened the door and said, "Good evening."

They saw a tall woman standing in the shadows of the front porch. She was wearing a suit with a long coat over a long skirt and an enormous black velvet hat with a drooping yellow plume. They could hear her saying, "Do forgive the intrusion."

"Care to step inside?" Mr. Swanson held the door open.

"Thank you, no," she answered. "My family is waiting for me."

He looked past her but could see no one. A flock of pigeons fluttered above the Smiths' porch across the street.

A harsh voice rang out in the house. "Hands up. I got a gun on you."

"I *beg* your pardon," the woman cried out, stepping back.

Mr. Swanson laughed. "That's the television. Maureen is watching a Western upstairs."

"A bracelet, priceless, was taken from our garden this afternoon by a child whom I followed up the street and saw turning in here."

Mr. Swanson called up the stairs. "Maureen, you come down here right this minute."

When Maureen saw the woman standing on her front porch, she felt a hot feeling in the pit of her stomach. It was Ingrid and she was staring so hard at her.

"That's the child." She nodded. Then she added, "Ugh."

"Beg pardon." Mr. Swanson was puzzled. "What did you say?"

"She," the woman went on, "took it from the garden at the Old Messerman Place."

Now if Ingrid had not said "Old Messerman Place," Maureen would have run upstairs, reached into the pocket of her sweater, hurried back down, and said, "Here. Here's your bracelet," and laid it in her hand.

But when she said "Old Messerman Place," Mr.

Swanson's face got stern and Mrs. Swanson's forehead creased with deep frowns.

"You did go there?" she asked Maureen.

"You've disobeyed me," said Mr. Swanson.

Maureen shouted, "I did *not*. I was *not*."

The woman on the porch was speaking in a low, well-modulated voice. "If my bracelet is returned, there will be no questions asked. If it is not"—and here she pulled down the brim of the big hat daintily—"there could be—unfortunate consequences."

Then she was gone. She was gone so suddenly it was as though when she stepped into the shadows cast by the trees near the walk, they had swallowed her up. Mr. Swanson looked up the street, expecting to see her walk into the light of the streetlamp at the corner. Mrs. Swanson looked in the other direction, thinking she might have walked to that corner to the bus. The sidewalks were empty. The woman in the old-fashioned clothes had vanished.

Mrs. Swanson was clearing the dinner table later that evening when she stopped suddenly and exclaimed, "Dad, look at that!"

He was reading the evening paper in the living room.

"There she is again, across the street, by the Smiths' porch."

He got up and looked out of the window. "That's not a woman. That's a tree by the Smiths' porch."

"Not the tree—next to the tree," she insisted, "between the tree and the house."

"Sure is," he nodded, "and what's she doing there, standing like a tree?"

Henry came in through the front door, his eyes wide.

"It's real weird," he told them, "that woman across the street. She keeps saying over and over, looking over here, 'Gimme my bracelet. Gimme my bracelet.' Listen to her."

They listened. In a monotone, low-pitched, over and over she repeated, "Give me my bracelet."

"You'd better have a talk with Maureen," Mrs. Swanson decided as she shut the door. "There's something about this I don't like."

Maureen, lying on her stomach on her bed and reading a copy of "Catman," had not noticed the three pigeons fluttering on the sill of her bedroom window. Even when Mr. Swanson came into the room, sat down on a little chair, and began to talk, she did not look up from the comic.

"I'll never forget," he began good-humoredly, "when I was a kid and a man came to our house and said I'd broken his window. I said 'no.' I lied."

Now Maureen raised her head. "So, what did they do to you?" she inquired with mild interest.

"Nothing," he answered. "They believed me, and the man went away. But in here"—and he held his hand by the pocket on the left side of his shirt—"there was a lot going on. In my heart I knew I'd lied and I lost my self-respect."

Maureen said nothing. Then he asked quietly, "Maureen, have you got something you'd like to tell me?"

She nodded, put down the comic, and stood up. The pigeons on the windowsill didn't make a sound.

"Okay." Mr. Swanson leaned back in the chair. "Let's have it."

"I need a new light for my bike," she told him. "Delbert Moody gunched my bike light. He stinks."

Mr. Swanson laid a dollar bill on the dresser and left the room.

She went now to her clothes closet, out of which she took a red sweater, found the feathered bracelet, and tried to slip it onto her wrist. It wouldn't go.

The pigeons cooed, flapped, and fluttered noisily on the windowsill. Maureen opened the window.

"Coo-coo yourself." She flapped her arms like wings. "Shoo-shoo." They flew away.

* * *

"Look there." Mrs. Swanson was pointing at the garage as she stood in the backyard. "Come out here, Dad, and look at these pigeons. See them? They're sitting there like painted or stuffed pigeons."

Mr. Swanson agreed. "Never saw pigeons act like that before." He lifted his arms and waved them back and forth. "Shoo-shoo."

The pigeons did not move. Their beady eyes looked into his steadily.

"Look there," Mrs. Swanson said as she pulled at his shirt, "look what's going on at the side of the house."

There stood Ingrid, looking up at Maureen's bedroom, her purse clutched in her hand. She was speaking through her teeth, in a monotone, saying over and over, "Give me my bracelet. Give me my bracelet. Give me my bracelet. . . ."

"Who's got what bracelet?" Mrs. Moody, next door, asked as she walked out on her porch, followed by Mr. Moody and Delbert.

"Nobody." Mr. Swanson crossed the lawn to speak to them. "The woman must be some kind of a nut."

Ingrid, hearing this, turned on her heel and walked rapidly across the yard and through the gate and down the alley.

Mrs. Moody couldn't believe her eyes. "Don't you know who that is?" She looked after her. "That's one of the Seven Slinky Sisters."

"The Seven Slinky Sisters?" Mrs. Swanson was astonished. "Who are they?"

"She and six other women dressed in funny old clothes like that shoplift pretty things in the stores in town. The police followed them once and saw them tossing things over the wall of the Old Messerman Place. Then they just disappeared."

"Disappeared?" Mr. Swanson's voice was puzzled. "How?"

Mrs. Moody didn't know.

"All I know," she went on, "is when they try to find them, they can't, and they can't find any of the things in there when they search. They watch and watch outside and nobody ever goes in there or comes out— except pigeons."

"That place is haunted, people say," Mrs. Swanson reminded her.

"It's weird, whatever it is," Mr. Swanson agreed. "And Maureen better never go anywhere near there."

Maureen didn't intend to go there. The next morning she carefully fitted the pigeon-feather bracelet into the sole of her shoe, between the bottom and the lining, planning to toss it over the wall of the Old Messerman Place on her way to school.

But she forgot.

THE HORSE-DRAWN CARRIAGE

That afternoon on the way home from school it began to rain. By the time Maureen was halfway home the rain turned into snow. She shivered, bowed her head against it, and ran.

An odd sound made her raise her head and look up. It was a clop-clop sound. She stepped back just in time as a shiny black carriage drawn by two gray horses moved in front of her.

A man with a whip in his hand, wearing a high silk hat and a long black coat, sat up high on a seat, and another man with a high hat and long black coat stood on a little step behind. Between them swung the black shiny body of the carriage. There were faces inside, but she couldn't see them clearly. What was *that*? She had never seen anything like it before except in picture books and movies. She ran after it.

Then she heard a clanging sound and saw two wide iron gates closing behind her. She pushed against them. They didn't move. They were locked tightly and they were so high. She remembered the gates at the Old Messerman Place, but she had never seen those without the boards behind. Those were rusty, but these were shiny black. Where was she?

She turned as she heard voices, and although there was now a thick curtain of snow, she dimly saw that people were getting out of the carriage and going into a big lighted house. Then the horses pulled the carriage away from the house and it rolled around the driveway toward her.

The man sitting up high with the whip had a thick mustache-like fringe. There were snowflakes on it. His face was red and his nose large. He was laughing now at something the man next to him was saying. This man had stood before on the step in the back of the carriage. They both saw her.

"Whoa," called the driver to the gray horses. "Whoa there."

They stopped. The driver leaned over. "What are you doing here," he asked her, "in this storm—half dressed?"

"You'll catch your death," said the second man.

She didn't answer. And she didn't know her mouth was open until she felt the taste of snowflakes on her tongue.

"Come into the stable and get warm," the driver said. Then he cracked the whip and the horses moved forward clop-clop-clop. Maureen followed them into a big brick building. There were stalls full of hay on one side and more hay in bins at the other side.

The men were taking the harnesses and bridles off the horses. The horses were tossing their manes and stamping their hooves. When they saw Maureen walking in, the men said gently, "Steady, girl, steady."

"Stand there by the stove," one told her, and pointed to a big round stove in a corner. It had a chimney and a bright metal skirt at the base. She had seen stoves like this in movies, too, and men with high hats like that and long coats like that in movies or old books. But she thought it was all "in the olden days" and nowhere around anymore.

"Where do you live, child?" one man asked her as he led the horses out of the shafts.

"331 Beach Street," she told him.

"Beach Street?" he repeated, puzzled. "Never heard of it. Must be in some other neighborhood."

"You're lost," the second one told her.

"Go to the kitchen door and ask for Nora. She'll take you home."

"Kitchen door? Where is the kitchen door?"

"There." And they pointed to a path outside the carriage house that stopped at steps leading up to a white wooden, screened-in porch.

She ran up the path against the snowflakes, but when she got to the door she stopped and looked around. She felt strange and timid.

The men called out to her. "Go on, knock on the door," they shouted. Then one of them said, "Nobody's gonna bite you." And they both laughed.

As she was raising her fist to knock, the door was opened and there stood a young woman wearing a long white apron over a long gray skirt. She had a puffed white starched hat on her head.

"Bless my soul," she said, and smiled. "Come on in and out of the storm—quick."

Maureen looked around the kitchen; big, warm, bright, cheerful—but different. There was no breakfast nook. The walls were painted yellow, the sink was shining like silver. The floor had blue and yellow linoleum. It made her think of something. She tried to remember something. The sink reminded her—of what? The young woman was pushing a high stool toward her.

"Sit yerself here," she said, smiling, "and I'll be bringing yez a glass of warm milk. It's like a drowned rat ye are."

She poured milk into a little pan, took it over to the stove, lifted the round black iron lid with a lever, and poked down inside. Maureen could see red-hot coals.

The young woman laughed. "Look at ye," she said. "Didn't you never see a coal range before?"

Maureen shook her head. "Only in an old house once."

"Have some cake." The maid handed her a plate with a piece of chocolate cake, a fork, and a neatly folded linen napkin. Maureen didn't want it and she didn't know why.

"No, thanks." She backed away. "I've got to get home."

"Where do ye live?"

"I live at 331 Beach Street."

She was like the men in the stable. "Never heard of it. Ye're sure that's it?"

Was she sure? Of course she was sure. She wrote it on every school paper: Maureen Swanson, 331 Beach Street.

"Wait here and eat that cake," the maid said as she smoothed out her apron, "and I'll ask the Missus where that is."

She left the room and Maureen followed her, holding the door open to see where she'd gone.

She gasped as she looked. It was so beautiful. Great, high-ceilinged rooms with lace curtains and velvet draperies tied back with gold ropes, a hall with a wide staircase going up, up, up. On the landing stood a tall grandfather clock with a round silver face and a long pendulum. This landing! It made her think of something, too. There was a landing on the stairs like that at the Old Messerman Place, but that was dirty and dusty. She looked into a big room with satin-covered sofas and chairs with gold legs, a black marble mantel where a fire burned, a handsome chandelier with candles, and a shiny black grand piano by the window. On the piano were two silver candelabra with five candles each. She tiptoed into the room and stood behind the piano. There was sheet music on it. One piece said: "Wait 'Til the Sun Shines, Nellie." Another said: "Moonlight Sonata." She could play chopsticks. She touched the keys now.

A voice called out, "How dare you?"

Maureen jumped.

Standing in the hallway were two little girls. One was her size, the other was taller, older. Both were wearing such funny clothes: long dresses, high shoes with buttons. Their hair was long and hung down their backs to their sashes.

The way they were looking at her! She might have been a bug. Such disgust was on their faces. She was startled at this look although she was used to people frowning at her, people who knew her, but she had never seen these girls before.

She got angry. "How dare *you*?" she shouted.

The little girls didn't flicker an eyelash. The taller one yawned and covered her mouth politely before she remarked in a cool voice to the younger one, "It talks."

"It!" They called her "it" as though she were a bug!

She ran toward them with her hand raised high to slap one of them, certainly the smaller one, more her size. But just then two more little girls came and stood next to them, then two more and finally a small one about five years old. Even this one wore a long dress and buttoned shoes.

"Look," said the tallest one as she waved toward Maureen, "what the wind blew in."

"You shut up!" Maureen was shouting, and there were angry tears in her eyes because all seven were now looking at her as though she were a bug and an "it."

They didn't seem to hear the shouting or see her upraised hand at all. They spoke to each other.

"What odd clothes," murmured one of them. "What an ugly voice," said another. "The silly shoes," said another. The one next to this one answered, as she giggled softly, "Shoes! Those can't be shoes!"

Then they all giggled, holding their hands over their mouths. Then the tall one stood up straight and took her hand off her mouth.

"Shh! She is coming."

A woman walked into the room now, followed by
the maid. The woman's hair was piled up high on her
head and fastened with two jeweled pins. Her dress fell
all the way to the floor. It was some kind of heavy wool
in a shade of gray. Earrings were set in her ears, matching a pin near her throat. Her eyes were so soft and
kind. She smiled at Maureen.

"Good afternoon, child," she said as she hurried
toward her. "Do you play the piano?"

The maid was frowning. "I told her to wait in the
kitchen, ma'am."

"Never mind, Nora." The mother's voice was soft.
"She wanted to see the house. Please play for us."

Then she sat down on the little satin sofa and
arranged her skirt neatly around her, and nodded to the
seven girls, who lowered themselves into other little
sofas and eyed Maureen as though she weren't there.
They were looking through her, or beyond her.

"Please play for us." The mother was waiting. Nora
stood in the hallway.

Maureen didn't want to play. She wanted to run away
from those seven girls who were regarding her now with
such amused, cold eyes. But the woman was smiling.

"Please, go ahead," she said, waving toward the
piano. Maureen sat down on the wooden stool and
played chopsticks. Then she stopped. She had heard

smothered giggles from the girls, who again held hands over their mouths.

"That's all I know," she told the woman, who smiled and clapped her hands.

"Very nice," she told her. "Keep on with your lessons."

"Mama." One girl stood up.

"May I play for *her*. She played for *us*."

"How kind!" The mother beamed. "Please do, Lucrece."

When Maureen heard that name, "Lucreesh," she wondered how you spelled it. It gave her an odd twinge in her mind to hear it. But this one was nothing at all like the "Lucreaky" she had seen in the painting at the Old Messerman Place. This one was only about eleven years old. She walked primly to the piano, spun the stool higher, sat down, arranged her skirt neatly, and placed her fingers on the keys.

Such music! It seemed to come like soft spring winds and soft summer nights—like a sprinkling, singing rain. It caught you and held you in a spell and you forgot where you were. Then it stopped. The woman leaned back, closing her eyes peacefully. The maid standing in the hallway was smiling, too. Now they all clapped their hands politely. Lucrece sat down on the sofa again, her head lowered modestly.

But the tallest sister glanced over at Maureen. "Don't you wish you could do that?"

"Shh," the mother said, frowning. "Someday she shall be able to play like that. Who knows?"

"Who knows?" echoed all the girls. Then they laughed softly as they stood on their feet.

"May we be excused, Mama?"

"Yes," she said, "but only to get your coats and bonnets and come with me in the carriage. As we drive this child home, we'll leave soup for old Mrs. Matthews."

Maureen saw the girls frown. "Again, Mama? We took soup to her *last* week."

"People get hungry every day," their mother reminded them. "Get into your coats and bring a warm shawl for this child. She is half dressed." They all filed out of the room.

Half dressed! Why did everyone say she was half dressed? She was dressed like all the other girls in her school: brown scuffs, short socks, a cotton dress, and a red sweater. They were dressed silly like old pictures: long dresses and high shoes with buttons! What kind of people were they? But she did like their mother.

The maid was pulling at the sleeve of her sweater. "You come now and wait in the kitchen." Out there she cried, "Look, now, and I've gone and scalded yer milk."

She held out the pan with slimy coating on top. As she poured it into a thick white cup she told her, "Ye're lucky, ye know. It's not all of 'em would hitch up the horses and drive ye home on a cold day, after just comin' in from one outing already."

It was crowded in the carriage. Four of the girls sat on one side, facing Maureen, the mother, and three others. Maureen, enveloped in a thick red shawl, was in a corner next to the mother. It was fun to hear the clop-clopping of the horses and feel the sway of the carriage itself, swinging gently back and forth, with a lullaby kind of movement, as though you were being rocked in a cradle by a gentle hand. How surprised her family would be when they saw the horses stop by the curb of the house on Beach Street. She hoped Henry and Diane would watch as she got out. She knew they would ask her all sorts of questions. Maybe Delbert Moody would see her, too, being handed out by the coachman who had handed her in. Maybe Junior Boggs and Baby would be watching from their windows, too. This thought made her happy. She leaned back and smiled and studied the faces of the sisters sitting across from her.

But she waited until they were *not* looking at her. Each wore a long woolen coat, buttoned all the way up to the chin. Each had her hands inside a little fur muff which matched the fur at the collar of her coat. Each wore a bonnet with a brim which curved. The brims were faced underneath with fluted silk which matched the linings of their coats. They still pretended to look past Maureen as though the corner of the swinging carriage were empty. Then she stopped looking at them and watched out the peephole kind of window of the carriage, through which she could see just by turning her head. The buildings looked so strange. None were tall. They all looked flat and squat.

There was a sign before one which said, "Feed and Grain." Another with a sign which read, "Thread and Notions." Another sign read, "Livery Stable." Another, "Saloon."

How strange it all was. She had never, never been in this part of her town before. The lamps on the street corners had odd shapes. Little bluish flames flickered inside the octagonal-shaped glass held with black iron bands. The way the people were dressed. All the women wore long skirts, the men high hats and some had coats with fur collars. *Where had she got to on the way home from school in the rain?*

Three times the horses stopped, and the man jumped off the back and went inside of a building to ask where Beach Street was. Three times he came back, shaking his head.

"They never heard of it here. It could be in the next town."

"How far did you come, child, do you remember?" the mother asked Maureen gently, for the tenth time.

She answered again the same way. "Just a few blocks. I was on my way home from school."

Did she see Lucrece now smile secretly at the tall sister sitting next to her? The smile they exchanged seemed to say, "We know something we won't tell."

They drove back to the big house.

Later, as Maureen was sitting on one of the satin chairs in the big room with the fireplace and the piano, she heard the mother say to someone in the hallway, "It's as though she had dropped out of the sky from some far-off place."

A big man wearing a coat with a fur collar came into the room and smiled at her. "Don't worry, young lady," he told her. "We'll get you home safely."

Then he turned to the mother. "Her parents are probably at the station house now looking for her."

No, thought Maureen, her parents never went to a station house. What was a station house? But they would be looking for her, calling all over the neighborhood, "Maureen! Maureen! Where are you?"

If they didn't find her, they would look for her in her bed and her dad would get out the car. What would those nasty girls think when they saw her dad driving up to those steps in a new blue Plymouth? Then she hoped it wouldn't happen because he would be so cross at her. Those girls would like that. No, she would find her own way home.

And now dinner would be served in ten minutes. Nora came in and told them and then took Maureen upstairs to a crazy kind of bathroom. The tub was a wooden box, lined with tin. The washbowl was gray marble, standing on iron legs. The john had a box above it, high against the wall. A chain with a wooden spool-like thing hung down from the side. You pulled this to flush it. There was no tile anywhere. The walls were wood and painted gray. The soap in the dish was yellow like a pumpkin. The bathroom at the Swansons' house was pink tile and the soap was perfumed. What if those girls could see that!

She was washing her hands and face as the knock came at the door and Nora handed in a long woolen dress. "Put this on."

Put that on! She would not. Oh, well, maybe just for fun, to try, but she wouldn't wear a heavy blue old thing like that. But she felt so grown-up and so different as she slid her arms into the long, wrist-length sleeves and buttoned the long dress. She felt cozy in it. It was chilly in the halls of this big house. And somehow it was like being in a school play. There was the sound of a bell outside—like chimes in a steeple.

"Dinner is served, miss," she heard Nora's voice call outside the door. Dinner is served, miss! She felt so big. They called her miss.

The dining room was beautiful. The candles flickered in the tall sticks. The wood on the walls glistened. The seven sisters sat all around the table, their hair combed neatly, brushed back from their foreheads and held with tiny black velvet ribbons across the head. The mother sat at one end. There was a vacant chair at the other end.

"Do we wait for the Mister?" Nora asked her.

"No. He will be late. He will dine when he returns and he asked us not to wait. Mr. Messerman has gone down to the station house."

"Mr. Messerman!" Maureen echoed, so surprised. "We live near the Old Messerman Place."

"The *old* Messerman Place!" Now it was the mother's turn to be surprised. "How strange! I had supposed we were the only family in town with that name. Where do you say this is?"

Maureen laid down her fork. "It's on my way home from school," she answered, noticing even then that the mother looked at her and listened, but the seven

sisters seemed to pay no attention, their heads lowered over plates, their forks moving up and down. "It's full of weeds and it's all boarded up and nobody lives there, except—"

The seven heads were now lifted and seven pairs of eyes were staring at her intently across the snowy linen cloth. The mother lifted a little brass bell. It went "tinkle-tinkle." Nora came through the swinging door from the kitchen, picked up a plate off the table, and carried it out.

"Except who?" the tallest girl prompted her.

"What?" asked Maureen. She had been watching Nora. When her mother cleared the table she picked up two dishes at one time.

"You said somebody lived—someplace," the tall girl repeated. "Where? Who?"

Maureen decided not to answer her. She looked at the mother and pointed to the walls of the room. "There's pictures like those. Castles and bridges and lots of girls with sheep. Only they're all dirty and when you hit them hard—does the dust ever fly—whew!"

"This tapestry was woven especially for us, we thought." The mother was eyeing the walls. Then she shrugged. "Apparently someone else ordered it also."

"There's a big thing like that." Maureen pointed across the hall toward the chandelier with the candles flickering. It looked like a birthday cake suspended from the ceiling. "But it's all hanging down now. Somebody swung on it, maybe."

Nora came back in and picked up another plate. She was carrying it out when Maureen said, "There's crazy pictures in the hall upstairs, pictures of ladies in long silk dresses."

The mother smiled fondly at her daughters. "Someday we plan to have our daughters' portraits painted."

Maureen didn't seem to hear her. "When they moved, they took out all the furniture except those seven pictures."

"Seven?—there?" The mother was so surprised again. "We have seven little ladies here," and she smiled at her daughters. "This is beginning to sound strange. Who *are* these people, I wonder?"

"Nobody," said the girl who played the piano. "She is making it up, Mama—to tease us."

"Please, Lucrece." And even though the mother looked at her fondly, she said firmly, "We must not be rude to our little guest."

Maureen was indignant. "I am *not* making it up. There's pictures of seven ladies in the upstairs hall of the Old Messerman Place. There's Cleo and there's Constance and there's Maude—"

Nobody was eating now. The mother wasn't even

smiling. Her eyes were fixed on Maureen, her fork was in midair, halfway to her mouth. But the seven sisters were all smiling. The tallest one spoke softly, "And Sylvia and Lucrece and Mavis and Ingrid."

"How did you know?" asked Maureen, after she had found her breath.

"Those are our names, silly." She smiled at her mother. "Mama, don't you see? She *is* making it up."

The mother hadn't moved her eyes from Maureen's face. And she wasn't smiling now. She looked frightened. She nodded. "Yes, Ingrid, I am afraid she is."

Maureen started to shout, but there was the sound outside of carriage wheels, voices raised, and then the thump-thump of somebody stamping snow off shoes. The big front door was flung open and the father came in, his cheeks red from the cold.

"Papa!" The seven daughters waved to him as he stood in the hall and handed his hat and gloves to Nora. The mother hurried to his side. Maureen heard him speaking in a low voice, but she couldn't hear what he said.

He waved at her, and smiled cheerfully. "Don't worry, child. Everything will be all right—tomorrow."

"Tomorrow!" She couldn't stay here till tomorrow.

She wiggled out of the big carved dining-room chair and ran toward the door, grabbing the knob.

"I got to go home." She was excited now. "They'll be looking for me."

But the father gently pulled her back. "You can't go out in that storm." His voice was kind, but firm. "I'd never forgive myself, little girl." Here he smoothed her hair with a big hand. "You must live in a neighboring town. Nobody at the station house ever heard of Beach Street."

"Papa." Ingrid was stroking the sleeve of his coat. "She knows where she lives and she knows how to get home, don't you?"

Maureen stepped closer to the big man as she saw the seven sisters moving toward her, smiling, not looking at her now as though she were a bug but as though they had known her before and disliked her. Then she heard it. It was a voice which seemed to come from somewhere upstairs. It was pitched low. It said, over and over, "Give me my bracelet. Give me my bracelet."

"Look!" The mother hurried to her side and took hold of her hand. "She is frightened at something, poor child."

The voice stopped. The lips of the seven sisters were curved in sweet smiles.

The father spoke. "Take her upstairs and put her to bed. The child is exhausted."

"Come with us." The tallest girl extended her hand.

"How sweet they are tonight!" Maureen heard the father's voice so full of happiness as he stood arm in arm with the mother and they beamed so proudly at the seven girls now moving toward Maureen.

"No! No!" she heard herself shouting. "No! No!"

Nora ran to her and took her hand.

"Let her come with me and the cook—up the back stairs. Sure she'll be fine there with us."

On the third floor, the rooms were small but cozy. They had low ceilings and they seemed to be snuggled in under the gables where the roof went slanting down. In the corner of the one where Nora took Maureen, there was a small pot-bellied stove with a bright fire inside. Through a window you could look in and see the flames. This window was not glass because glass would crack.

"It's what they call isinglass," Nora explained. "A special kind of thing that won't crack and melt like window glass."

Then she stopped buttoning the long white flannel nightgown with the long sleeves she had found for Maureen.

"Sure now, don't yez have a stove like that in your house?"

Maureen shook her head.

"Then how do yez keep warm on cold nights?"

"We have a big furnace in the basement. It's gas—I think."

"A what?" Nora echoed. "That's nothin' I ever heard of. Sure'n you must live a long ways from here. Now get into that bed there." She pointed to a small iron bedstead against the wall, piled high with blankets and a fat quilt. "It's nice to lie in the dark and watch them flames in that stove makin' things come onto the walls."

Maureen slid into the bed and shivered. The sheets were so cold!

"Here's yer pig," Nora said, laughing and watching her. Then she slid something between the sheets at the foot of the bed. It was a flat jug of hot water, stoppered tightly with cork and wrapped in a piece of flannel. Against Maureen's feet, it felt so warm and cozy.

"Look at yez." Nora laughed again. "One would think ye'd never even seen a pig before. I wonder where you come from, sure?"

Then she blew out the candle, set the candlestick on the top of a small chest, and went to the door.

"Don't go." Maureen sat up in the bed. "Stay here."

The flames from the little stove were dancing shapes up and down the walls. It was a whispering kind of a room now. Maybe that was why Nora whispered as she stole back to the bed and gently pushed Maureen down onto the pillow. "Don't mind *them*," she whispered.

"Stick close to the mother and father. They're the *good* ones." She smoothed her hair, kissed her forehead, and left the room.

Maureen lay in the little bed and watched the firelight from the stove dancing on the walls. Through the window she could see white stars outside. Where was she? How could she have got lost—so far—and found herself in a house with gaslight, candles, stoves like this, horses in a stable, no television, no telephone? Telephone! They must have a telephone. Everybody had a telephone. Why hadn't she said right away, "Call my dad. Our number is 345-1212."

She jumped out of bed. She'd call him now. He'd come for her in their car. He'd be cross at her for not phoning before. Then she remembered why she hadn't told them to phone.

She had meant to say it when she heard them say "tomorrow," but the voice up the stairs whispering "Give me my bracelet" had frightened her so she'd forgotten.

No, it was before that she first became uneasy— when the seven daughters told their names at the dinner table. The uneasiness came over her again now. How could they have the same names as the pictures in the upstairs hall of the Old Messerman Place?

Then she smiled. It was a dream. She was dreaming it

all. She would go back to bed and when she woke up she would hear the television downstairs or the radio blaring in the breakfast nook in the kitchen or Henry and Diane arguing. She smiled again and got back into bed.

When her feet touched the warm "pig" she jumped out again. How could you dream about things you'd never seen or heard about? Not even on TV or in the movies or books? There must be a telephone.

Looking out of the door, she couldn't see anything in the darkness. She found a box of matches beside the candlestick, lit the candle, and held it firmly. In its light she could now see a narrow hall and steps going down into the kitchen.

The phone at home was in the kitchen. She went slowly, quietly down the steps, came to a small hall with two doors, opened one, and found herself in a large, wide hallway with doors like a hotel hall. The carpet was thick under her bare feet. This wasn't the way to the kitchen. She had opened the wrong door. This led to the wide front staircase with the banister and the landing with the lace curtains and the clock.

Then she heard a murmur of voices. Somebody else was up. The voices were low and sweet. The mother and father talking together somewhere.

Peeking around the corner of the wall at the stairs,

she almost dropped the candlestick. At first it looked like a crowd of ghosts on the landing. There was a rush of cold air. The sisters, in long white gowns, were gathered by the open window looking out and talking to somebody outside. They were saying softly, "Pretty, pretty, pretty."

Who could they be talking to, leaning over, heads lowered?

She couldn't see. Then she heard wings flapping and saw something flutter down. Pigeons! The sisters were talking to a flock of pigeons on the sill of the window at the landing.

A door opened down the hall. Voices rang out. Maureen stepped back, blew out her candle, and waited.

Two candles flickered at the other end of the long wide hall. The father and mother were coming. She was in a long nightgown with sleeves and ruffles, a cap on her head. He was in a long nightshirt, with a cap on his head, which flipped over to one side. They looked like a picture she had once seen in a book of *"The night before Christmas and all through the house—"*

The seven sisters clustered together on the landing raised their eyes to their parents, who were looking so surprised at the top of the stairs.

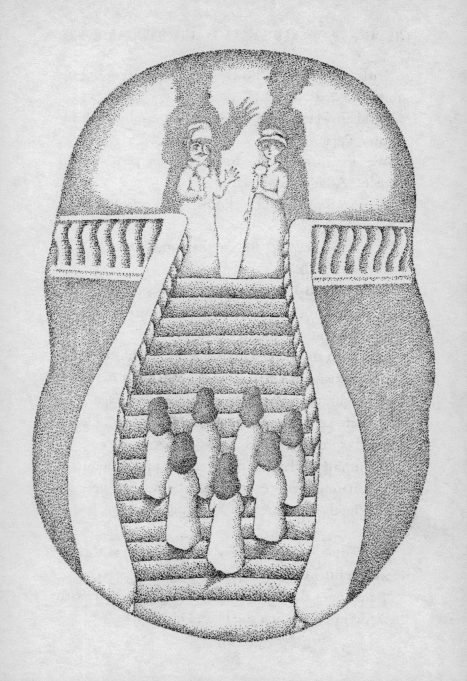

"Girls," asked their father, "what are you doing up out of your beds at night?"

Ingrid answered, "We got up to get ourselves a drink of water, Papa."

"We are so sorry we disturbed your rest," added Lucrece. "Aren't we, sisters?"

The sisters all said in a chorus, "So sorry, dear Papa and dear Mama."

"You'll catch cold," the mother said, worried. "Go back to your beds."

"Nora should have put pitchers of water in their rooms," the father grumbled. "They must not wander around the house at night."

The seven sisters filed up the stairs. Each one raised on tiptoe, kissed her father's cheek, then her mother's. "Good night, dear Mama. Good night, dear Papa."

As each went into her bedroom, she turned, blew a kiss, and closed the door.

"Charming." The big man put an arm around his wife. "Charming girls even if they did wake us up."

The mother frowned. "Charming, yes—but sometimes—"

"Sometimes—what?" His voice was gruff, as though he were a little cross with her.

"Sometimes they can be heartless. They were with the little lost girl when she played chopsticks."

"Nonsense." The father did not like this. "They're young and thoughtless, maybe—but heartless, never. Come back to bed."

Maureen watched the two candles moving down the hallway. She heard a door close. She was in darkness now except for the light from the landing window, pale and cold as it flowed down the broad staircase like a waterfall, swallowed up by the darkness of the hall downstairs. She felt cold and lonely as she crept toward the stairs.

The sound of voices from behind a bedroom door stopped her and she ran back down the hallway. They were coming out again, she knew, to talk to the pigeons. Feeling her way along the wall, she came to a door, opened it, and found herself in the little hall of the back stairs. She crept up to the room with the little stove. As she turned the knob, a voice called out, "Who's there?"

A fat woman in a nightgown and cap was sitting up in the little bed, her hand over her mouth. "Oh, it's you," she scolded. "Your room's the one next door. Go back to bed."

It was the cook, Lizzie. Maureen had met her in the kitchen before dinner, and she was so mad. It made Maureen feel much better. Even though she wasn't home, when people scolded her she felt at home. She got into the bed and her feet felt for the pig. It was not warm now. As she laid her head down on the pillow and pulled the covers up tightly over her head, she told herself she didn't know where she was or how she got there but she was sure now—it wasn't a dream and she would find a telephone somewhere tomorrow.

HOW TO GET HOME AGAIN

The next morning, when Maureen woke up and looked around, the fire had gone out in the potbellied stove in the corner. She shivered. The stove looked dreary and forgotten. Last night it had seemed so cheerful and happy, blazing away with the flames behind the window Nora had called isinglass. Now she noticed that it sat on a square piece of painted tin, and that cold ashes had spilled out of a small iron door near the bottom of the stove itself onto the tin square. She remembered, in a flash, everything from the night before. Those crazy girls talking to pigeons when she went to look for a telephone. Telephone! She'd better find one quickly. Her mother and father would be so mad!

Why didn't you call? Where were you? We waited dinner. We went all over the neighborhood calling you.

She could hear herself telling them, *It was a big house with lots of people. They have horses, but no car. They never heard of Beach Street. They made me stay.*

89

She knew she wouldn't say this. She would shout, *I don't know. Leave me alone. You blame* me *for everything.*

The door opened and Nora stood there grinning. "What's all the shoutin'. Ye'll wake the dead."

"Where's the telephone?" Maureen jumped out of bed. The floor beneath her feet was icy cold.

"Where's the what?" Nora looked puzzled.

"You know—the telephone," Maureen repeated patiently. "Telephone! You know, where you think of somebody and then dial a number and pretty soon the person you dialed says 'hello' right in your ear."

Nora was staring at her, shaking her head slowly back and forth. "I never seen nothin' like that."

"That's silly, everybody's got a telephone," Maureen insisted, "and a television, too."

"A what?"

"A television. Look . . ." Maureen felt so grown-up now and older than Nora, who was a woman. She made the shape of a box with her two hands as she explained, "It's a box about so big. You turn on a switch and you see people in it about so big. They're talking to you and singing and dancing. You can see them, but they can't see you."

She heard a crash and saw the pitcher Nora had in her hands go crashing down to the floor, water spilling all over, and Nora running out of the room. How Maureen laughed.

The door opened again and there stood Lizzie, the cook, in a white apron and cap. Nora was behind her.

"Tell her." Nora indicated Lizzie with her hand. "She won't believe me."

"Tell her what?" asked Maureen.

"What you told me—where you get 'hello' in the ear and see little people in a box talking and singing and dancing."

Maureen told it again. Lizzie backed away from her and made the sign of the cross over herself. They both backed out of the room, watching her all the while.

Even though their voices were pitched low in the hall outside, Maureen, close to the door now, could hear every word they said.

"She's a devil." That was Lizzie's voice in a thick whisper. "And she's come here to us because of them and they're devils, too, always with the birds and plottin' mischief among themselves."

"She's lyin', maybe," said Nora. "Making up things, like Miss Ingrid said last night at dinner."

"That one would know another liar all right," Lizzie's voice answered. "She's a liar herself, and no mistake."

"What do we do?" asked Nora.

"If she's a devil," Lizzie's voice came slowly, "I'm not spendin' another night in this house. If she's a liar, I'll give her a swat on the rump with the rough side of my hand."

Maureen got away from the door and was standing beside the bed as Lizzie marched in again, Nora behind her.

"You was lyin'," demanded Lizzie, "wasn't you?"

Maureen was never quite sure what made her nod her head. Was it because she knew it would make them both happier or was it because she had been called a liar so often? Or was it because this morning, with the broken pitcher on the cold floor, the cold ashes on the tin platform below the cold little stove, and the two women in starched caps and aprons glaring at her, something inside her told her not to insist on the telephone or television? She nodded.

They both smiled, even though the smiles were grim, with no happiness in them.

"I knew it." Lizzie came toward her. "I could tell by the look in yer eyes." Then she gave her a hard slap across the lower back. Tears welled up into Maureen's eyes, and for the first time in her life she dropped her head and sobbed. She didn't stamp her feet or clench her fist or shout.

"Stop that," Lizzie scolded, "stop that cryin' and get washed for breakfast, and no more lies."

While Nora swept the pieces of the broken pitcher into a dustpan, Maureen got into the long woolen dress again, because Nora said so. She almost cried once more as she saw her own cotton dress, socks, and sweater lying on the little chair by the bed. She was starting to pull on her own socks and shoes when Nora handed her a pair of ugly long black stockings and a pair of high shoes with buttons.

"Wear these," she ordered, and handed her a metal rod with a hook at the end. "And here's a buttonhook."

Maureen was looking at it wonderingly as Nora knelt down on the floor before her. "Hold out yer foot."

Then she deftly pushed the little hook through the buttonholes on one side of the shoe, twisted it around the buttons, and in and out to the top until both shoes were buttoned high around her legs. They felt tight and strange.

"Downstairs, now!" She got up. "The family's waitin' breakfast." Her voice was not unkind anymore.

Some of the family had finished breakfast. As she came down the front hall, she could see the sisters being handed into the carriage, which waited at the porch steps. The man with the whip was sitting high on the seat again. The other man was helping the sisters to get inside. They were wearing, this morning, long brown woolen coats with brown velvet buttons and brown velvet-brimmed hats.

93

"The young ladies are off to the young ladies seminary," Nora said from the step above her. "Ye slept late. Have breakfast in the kitchen."

Maureen was so glad she would not have to see those sisters.

As she sat on a stool in the kitchen, eating pancakes with thick syrup, she heard Nora and Lizzie whispering together in a room with glass-doored cupboards next to the kitchen. They called this "the butler's pantry."

"The Mister is gonna look for her family today in the next town, Cedar Hill."

Maureen wanted to cry out, "Cedar Hill. I don't live in Cedar Hill." She knew where that was. She had been there often. The Swansons often drove to Cedar Hill on a Sunday in the car. But she said nothing.

She watched them, lifting a round lid off the stove, putting wood into the hole and then coal, as they heated water and washed the dishes in a big tin pan, drying them carefully on soft white cloths. At the sound of a tinkling bell from the dining room, Lizzie would say, "That's him," or "That's her," and hand a silver tray to Nora which held a glistening cut-glass bottle of syrup. Nora would smooth her apron, fix her cap, put a smile on her face, take the tray, and walk through the swinging door into the dining room.

As Maureen was studying the pattern of the linoleum

on the kitchen floor, she seemed to see it grow dusty and dirty and faded. She seemed to see it crack open, become a big hole through which she could see old trunks with leather handles, striped with tin. Then she saw a black cat leap up through the hole and spring onto the drainboard of the sink. She cried out.

"What's that for?" Lizzie demanded, coming close to her. Then the floor was clean, with no hole, and there was no cat on the drainboard. The fire was crackling in the stove and Nora was back with the silver tray.

"What's the matter?" she asked Lizzie.

"She let out a yelp, all of a sudden," Lizzie explained. "Now why did you do that?"

"I saw . . . ," Maureen began.

"Saw what?" Lizzie was looking so cross.

"Nothing," she answered.

"Eat your breakfast and no more yelping. After breakfast you can walk about the place. The sun's out today."

"Where—where is she?" Maureen asked suddenly.

"'She'—'she' is the cat's grandmother," Lizzie told her, and Maureen looked at the drainboard quickly.

"Don't never say 'she.'" Nora was shaking her forefinger at her. "Say the name you mean. That's more ladylike."

"I mean—their mother," Maureen answered after a wait.

"Mrs. Messerman? She's busy. Why?"

"She's nice!" Maureen's voice was soft.

Their faces softened now.

"Ye'll never find no one nowhere that's nicer," Nora said, and turned her face away. "And it's the devil's own shame she has such . . ."

"Shh," warned Lizzie. "Little pitchers have big ears."

Maureen went out the back door wearing a long woolen coat which clung to her ankles as she walked in the high-buttoned shoes. It was the kind of a coat you had to walk in. You couldn't run. The sun had come out. All the snow was gone from the grounds except the little patches lying in the shade of the house itself, where the sun couldn't find them. Maureen walked around to the stables, now empty. What an awful smell! She didn't go inside, but turned now and wandered through the big garden and across the closely cropped lawns.

She looked everywhere, into little corners and along little paths bordered with flower beds. Coming out of one clump of trees, she couldn't believe her eyes. There stood the iron boy, holding the fish over the pond. But now paint wasn't peeling off his arms. He was painted a bright fresh green on his iron jacket, his cap was red, his short pants bright blue. His face was painted pink, his lips red, and his eyes blue. He looked beautiful. She ran to him and felt his arm. His iron eyes looked vacantly into hers when she leaned over and held her face close to his. She almost fell into the water of the pond, now clear except for a patch of ice coating here and there, when she heard a tap-tapping sound. She didn't fall because she held on to the arm of the iron boy. Turning slowly, she saw a summerhouse, painted white and green, a white bench nearby on the wet grass. Tap-tap-tap!

He was there. And he was sitting on a pile of clean new canvas. The birdbath wasn't there, and the coiled hose in the corner wasn't peeling. It was shiny and black. The leprechaun looked just the same. He was wearing the brown knitted cap, the dusty shirt, and the canvas pants. One cheek was puffed out, and he spat out a nail with a "pish" sound as he lifted the hammer and went tap-tap-tap on the sole of the shoe.

"So it's you," he said, not looking up. "And didn't I tell yez yesterday to go away from here and not come back?"

"Yesterday," she echoed. "Yesterday it was snowing."

"How the weather does change. Now ye're Maureen Messerman."

"No, no," she cried. "I'm Maureen Swanson and I live at 331 Beach Street." Then she stepped closer to him and whispered, "What happened?"

It was a half a minute before he stopped pounding.

"You had the wish and they had the time. They got that out of my bag of tricks—them thieves."

"I want to go home. How can I get home?"

"Why do yez want to go home from a fine place like this?" His blue eyes were looking into hers now, not blinking.

"Because," her voice was breaking, "because nobody slaps me there," and she didn't add, "I slap them." She said out loud, "I want to go home; they treat me like a bug here. Oh, please tell me—how can I get home?"

"Yer dreamin', you know," he told her. But she couldn't believe that.

"Dreaming! When you dream, you're in bed asleep."

"That's what you think," he said, laughing, "but here's what you do to get home."

Just then she heard Nora's voice calling to her and then Nora herself running into the summerhouse.

"Don't come in here." Nora looked around nervously, and then sighed with relief first before she put the question, "Did you see anyone at all in here?"

The leprechaun lifted his head from behind the pile of hose and put his little brown finger to his lips.

"No," she answered. Nora pushed her out. "And don't be comin' here anymore."

The iron gates were swinging wide open, pulled apart by the footman, who had jumped off the back step of the carriage. The horses trotted past the summer-house and three faces with brown velvet bonnets glared at her through the carriage windows. The carriage stopped at the house and the sisters were handed out. They ran, laughing, up to the door and Cleo reached out her hand to grasp the knob.

But Maude laid a gloved hand on her sister's. "Wait," she told her coldly. Then she looked at the footman, who said, "Yes, miss," and pushed open the door.

Ingrid was now looking across the garden at Maureen. "That vile child is wearing Mavis's coat." Her voice rang out. "And she does not have it buttoned properly."

The door closed. The sisters were home for lunch.

"Come in now," said Nora, "and have lunch with the young ladies."

"No." Maureen didn't budge. She dug the thick heels of the high shoes deep into the wet ground. "I won't. I'm going home." She had seen the gates—now open.

She ran across the lawn, out of the gates, and down the walk outside toward home—not noticing that it wasn't a paved walk but a dirt path she was on.

Somehow she had gotten into the Old Messerman Place when it was the *new* Messerman Place, something she had often dreamed of doing. But the seven ladies in the pictures-that-moved in the dusty upstairs of the *Old* Messerman Place being here now as young girls in the *new* Messerman Place was something she could never have even imagined.

It had fine furniture now and curtains and cooking in the kitchen and horses in the stable, but it was the same place. She had been sure of that as soon as she saw *him. What did he mean you could be dreaming without being asleep in bed?*

She was running fast, her coat making her stumble and fall twice in the muddy ground. Where were all the houses?

At the corner where she always turned on the way home from school there was vacant ground with weeds. As far as her eyes could see there were no houses. Had the Swansons' house been there? She couldn't be sure. How could you tell with everything stretching away—empty?

There was a house! She was happy to see it, though she didn't remember it. It was yellow brick, with a small white porch with white wooden curlicues under the roof like paper cutouts. A sign said: "Music Lessons." She pounded at the door. Maybe they had a telephone.

The door was opened by a thin little woman. She had a thimble on one finger. She was wearing a long black dress. She looked suspiciously at Maureen and latched the screen.

"What do *you* want?"

"I'm lost," Maureen gasped, "and I want to get home."

"Where did you come from?" the woman asked her.

"I was coming home from school and I saw a carriage with horses. Can I use the phone?"

"The what?" Her eyes widened. "Can you use— what?" Then Maureen saw her looking past her at someone or something.

The carriage was standing outside, with the horses stamping and tossing their manes. The sisters looked out of the window. Ingrid got out.

"She's lost." Ingrid smiled at the music teacher as she took hold of Maureen's elbow. "But she *does* know how to get home."

The woman closed the door, and Maureen heard the sound of a bolt drawn across it.

She got into the carriage, where Lucrece, Constance, and Mavis were seated languidly against the cushions.

Ingrid leaned back into the carriage. "You know how to get home?" she smiled, and said after a while.

"You know?" echoed the others.

"No, no, I don't." Her voice was tearful as the carriage stopped before the steps and the mother came out of the door.

"Child," she said gently, "you mustn't run away again. You might get lost—more and more."

That night, after dinner, she told herself she would wait in the little room upstairs until everybody was asleep and then, when the house was dark, get out of bed and find the leprechaun again in the summerhouse.

But the mother took her hand and said, "In the drawing room we shall have music whilst we wait for Mr. Messerman to return with word from your parents."

That was a strange word, "whilst," instead of while, but Maureen didn't mind it. She didn't mind anything the mother said or did. She was always sweet, gentle, and patient.

She held Maureen's hand as they sat on a little satin-covered sofa, and Lucrece played for them. Tonight she didn't play the soft rain kind of music but a sprightly, happy popular tune. The girls gathered around the piano and sang. Then Nora and Lizzie and the two men from the stable stood in the hall and sang, too. The words they sang were:

Wait 'til the sun shines, Nellie, and the clouds go rolling by.
We will be happy, Nellie, don't you cry.
Wait 'til the sun shines, Nellie, and the clouds go rolling by.
We will be happy, Nellie—bye and bye.

There was something so sad about those words—"bye and bye." She thought of home. They would all be watching television after dinner. Henry would want cartoons, Diane would want music, her dad, the news.

Her mother would be in the kitchen, stacking the dishes in the dishwasher, reminding them all, "Don't quarrel, children. Someday you will be thousands and thousands of miles from each other."

She felt the taste of salt on her lips and knew then tears were rolling down her cheeks. Nobody noticed. Everybody was singing and smiling. Who were these people? How had she got here? The song was like a bridge, taking her thoughts home.

Her heart was breaking.

The door opened. Mr. Messerman stepped inside and motioned to his wife, who joined him in the hallway.

Maureen knew before he spoke what he would say.

"There's no Wilbert Swanson in Cedar Hill. We'll put an ad about her in the paper tomorrow, and if that doesn't work . . ."

He whispered in his wife's ear, and she nodded. Then she said, "How sad it must be for them to have their daughter go away and not come back!"

Here the mother's eyes rested on her own daughters, sitting in the big room. She shivered. She must be cold, Maureen decided.

She was sitting in the chair in the little room on the third floor next to Nora's. The stove was crackling with a fire when the door opened. Thinking it was Nora, she began to get into bed. It wasn't Nora tonight, holding a candlestick. It was the mother. Her face looked so

sad. She sat on the bed, next to Maureen, and smoothed her hair.

"I saw you crying tonight," she said gently.

"I want to go home." Maureen put her hands to her eyes.

"I know," she said, nodding. "And we'll advertise in the papers beginning tomorrow. But if we shouldn't hear, I want you to know—you can live here with us. You can be Maureen Messerman, and I will have eight daughters."

Maureen lifted her head. "No," she said. "I want to go home." And then she cried.

The mother hugged her. "Don't," she said to comfort her, "don't." Then she was silent, before she spoke in a faraway tone—as to the air. "My daughters never cry. I wonder why not?"

"Maybe," Maureen said, speaking slowly, "because they're always happy."

The mother shook her head back and forth. "No, that's not it."

She got up and went to the door, then stopped, and impulsively turned around and ran to Maureen. "You!" She was looking at her so pleadingly. "If you can ever help them—will you do it—please?"

"Me?" Maureen had never been so amazed in all of her life. "Me—help them?" Her help anybody? Nobody had ever said that to her before. She looked up into the mother's anxious face, now fastened on hers. Didn't she know Maureen was the Stinky Swanson everybody ran away from? The one nobody played with, the one always kept after school. No, the mother didn't know about her. That's why she asked her this—as though—as though—she were somebody else. Of all the strange sensations she had had since she followed the carriage, this was the most astonishing. She was not only far from home, she was even far from herself. She looked into the mother's eyes and nodded her head slowly, feeling, somehow, like a cheat. With pity she watched her go out of the room.

She was in bed, lying with her face downward on the pillow, when she knew somebody had come into the room. She didn't move. By the light of the moon, she could see white fingers moving near her head. She lay very still. Then from the corner of her eye she could see them feeling in the pocket of her red sweater, hanging on the chair by the head of the bed. The fingers felt in both pockets. There was no sound of a door closing or feet moving across the floor, but she knew whoever had come in had gone out. When she was quite sure of this, she sat up in bed. Somebody was standing in the outside hall.

Then she heard it. At first she didn't understand the words clearly. As she listened and listened, she edged back more in the bed to get away from it, edged until her back was against the iron head of the bed and her own head against the wall.

The voice was saying, "Give me my bracelet. Give me my bracelet. Give me my bracelet."

She heard another voice shouting. A second later she knew it was herself. "Take your old bracelet."

She waited for the door to open and grown-up Ingrid to come inside. How she could be here, Maureen didn't know, but that was the voice that had called up to the bedroom that time by the side of the Swansons' house.

The door *did* open now, but it was Lucrece, Maude, and young Ingrid, not the woman in the suit with the long coat and the black hat with a drooping plume. Each wore a long white ruffled nightgown and each carried a flat silver saucer-type candleholder with one candle set in the center. They looked so anxious and so sweet.

"What's wrong, little girl?" Maude glided over to the bed.

Then Nora, tying a cord around a long wrapper, pushed past Maude and Lucrece. "What's goin' on here with yez?" she asked crossly. And she put a hand on Maureen's forehead.

"A bad dream, poor child," said Lucrece.

"Poor child." Maude and Ingrid smiled.

"She'll wake up the Mister and Missus." Then Nora's face softened. "Is it sick ye are, child?" she asked her kindly.

Maureen shook her head and grabbed hold of Nora's hand. "Don't go, don't go," she whispered, her eyes on the three girls, lined up like three ghosts at the foot of the little iron bed.

"Go back to bed, Nora." Ingrid was smiling. "We'll sit with her until she goes back to sleep."

"We'll tell her a sweet story, won't we, Maude?"

"And say her prayers with her." Lucrece smiled.

Nora felt Maureen's hand clutching her own, tighter and tighter. She studied them, the three girls standing there, looking so kind, gentle, and concerned, their gowns as white as snow, their hair soft and yellow falling down their backs.

But she said, "Young ladies need their rest. Sure you run on back to yer own beds and I'll sit here with the child awhile." She waited for them to leave.

Ingrid could make her voice as cold as an icicle, the sharp pointed kind, with the end like a needle. "That's kind of you, Nora, but you need your rest for your work here. Good night—and goodbye."

"Goodbye?" echoed Nora. "And why are ye sayin' goodbye at this time of night, I'd like to know?"

"You'll see." Ingrid opened the door.

"There's somethin' goin' on here," Nora told them, her voice rising. "Late or not late, I'm wakin' up the folks. You stay there till I come back." She pointed a stern finger at Maureen.

They could hear her running down the hall, doors slamming in the passageway.

Lucrece closed the door and leaned against it while Ingrid asked quietly, "Where is it?"

"Here!" She picked up the shoe and, as they watched intently, she pried out the pigeon-feather bracelet and handed it to Ingrid. "I found it on the grass."

Ingrid didn't hear. She slipped it onto her wrist. Her eyes glittered and her voice throbbed with excitement. "Freedom, sisters!" She laughed. "Freedom again. The sky is mine tonight. Let us fly westward."

"Westward," they echoed, "westward—forever." And they ran to the door.

"Wait," Maureen cried, "wait, wait."

Ingrid turned. "Wait? For what?" Her eyebrows were raised in surprise. "To say 'thank you' for returning what was mine, what I had to go to so much trouble to get back and take so much time."

As she said "time," she smiled mysteriously. "Come, sisters."

And again they moved to the door.

Maureen was frantic now. "Wait—please. Get me—back home again."

Lucrece seemed so surprised. "I—I am—too *fooey*. Perhaps Maude."

Maude couldn't seem to believe her ears. "I—but I *stink*. You do it, Ingrid."

"I?" Ingrid didn't smile at all. She glared at Maureen. "I—am too *ugh*. Come, sisters." She went to the door.

"Wait," Maureen cried out after them, "I'm sorry I called you bad things. Get me home—please!"

They didn't hear. They didn't stop. She could hear them running down the back stairs, calling the others. "Cleo, Mavis, Constance, Sylvia. Hurry! Hurry!"

"Hurry!" Maureen dressed herself so fast. She would follow them. They must get her home. Oh, why had she called them bad names?

Into the underwear, dress over the head, on with the socks, now into the brown scuffs, arms into the sweater, and into the hall.

She could hear the sound of running feet everywhere, voices calling out, and doors slamming.

The sisters were running down the wide stairs of the front hall toward the door.

"Quick," Ingrid urged them, "before they find us."

After Ingrid came Maude, Lucrece, Cleo, Constance, Mavis, and the smallest one, Sylvia.

"Wait." Maureen was breathless. "Wait—get me home."

"Girls! Girls! Where are you going? Stop!"

They all stopped. Maureen looked up to see Mr. Messerman, halfway down the stairs after them, holding his candlestick close to his astonished face. The mother stood on the landing between Nora and Lizzie. Lizzie's hair hung in two gray braids. The daughters, all except Ingrid, stood in a row in the hall, their heads bowed, their arms at their sides in their snowy white gowns. Maureen's eyes were on the mother's face, so sad and anxious. She saw her shake her head as if saying "no, no" as Ingrid took one step up the stairs, then stopped. Ingrid raised one white arm up high, then brought it down quickly, like a slash cutting the air.

There wasn't a sound. Darkness settled on the hallway. The moonlight poured in through the lacy curtains on the landing with the clock. The clock ticked. No one was standing in the hall. No one was standing on the stairs. Had they ever stood there at all? Maureen wondered all of her life.

She was wondering as she went out the front door. The garden was still and beautiful in the moonlight, the lawns closely clipped, the bricked driveway swept clean. She ran across the lawn to the high iron gates.

They were locked! Through palings she could see

the streetlamps dotting the road ahead out there, getting smaller and smaller in the distance. A carriage was rolling along, drawn by two black horses, only one man in the high seat. People inside were laughing. A man looked out the window and smiled at the little girl shaking the gates, crying out, "Let me out. Let me out."

Then she remembered. She raised her arm high and brought it—slash—down through the air. Nothing happened. The gates didn't swing open. The street with the lamplight, the rolling carriage, and the laughing voices were still there. She did it again. Nothing happened.

The voices in the carriage grew fainter and fainter. Then everything was still. She was locked back here in the "olden days" garden and there was no nice Nora in the house now, nor Lizzie, nor Mr. Messerman, and no nice mother. She was all alone!

She jumped suddenly as she heard a flutter-flutter sound. Seven pigeons huddled on the roof of the house watching her. Only pigeons! She threw herself onto the ground and sobbed and kicked and screamed.

A voice at her ear said, "Soft pedal. Ye'll wake the dead."

It was the leprechaun, crouching down beside her.

"I can't get home. I gave her back her bracelet and I'll never get home again."

"Ye might," he told her, stroking his beard with his small brown hand. "Pretend is tricky business—but *un*pretend, that's even trickier."

"*Unpretend*," she repeated. "How?"

"So what's going on at home now?" he asked her.

"At home now? Oh! Well! They'd be out looking for me. I'd be hiding from them. My mother would be so mad. She'd be calling me, she'd be . . ."

"Show me," he said. "I'm slow to catch on to some things."

"I'd be like this," she answered, crouching down behind something that wasn't there, hiding from a mother who wasn't coming.

"And she'd be like this, coming up the street, her feet going like this. . . ."

Now she folded her arms across her chest, walked with a hard stomp, and called in a sharp voice, "Maureen! Maureen! You get home."

A chilly wind blew over the garden. The stars seemed to stand still. From someplace, somehow, a cross voice rang out through the night air of the "olden days" garden.

"Maureen! Maureen! Where are you?"

A light came up from somewhere, like a switch turned on. She was all alone again and a windy rain was falling on the dusty, littered steps of the Old

Messerman Place. The windows were dark and dirty, without curtains. The screen on the door was moving and whining in the wind. The iron boy by the pond was weather-beaten, paint peeling off his arms. There were no pigeons on the roof. She heard a purring sound outside, beyond the boarded-up gates. It was the sound of cars moving toward the intersection. She heard the voices of children running down a sidewalk. That was Delbert Moody, calling out to Junior Boggs, "Paper drive tomorrow. Don't forget the paper drive!"

"Paper drive tomorrow!" That was what the teacher had said to her as she left school in the rain—when? Had it all happened that afternoon, within an hour, maybe?

She walked slowly back to the house. There was the clean spot in the dusty window on the landing where she'd last seen the lace curtains and the tall grandfather clock. She went slowly into the kitchen through the swinging doors where Nora had carried the plates, one at a time. There was the big hole in the linoleum and the old trunks piled in the cellar below, the blackened tin sink, the pail of water, half filled, which Delbert had dragged in from the back porch the other day. The castles and bridges and the girls and lambs on the wall of the dining room were dim and dusty again. She remembered how the girls' skirts had been red. Was it only a night or two ago? An hour ago? Or ever? She didn't know. But it was now so faded you couldn't guess what color they had been. And yet she did know. The color had been red, had always been meant to be red.

In the drawing room, as they'd called it, there was the chandelier hanging by one wire. The black piano had stood there by the wide window with the velvet drapes, gold ropes, and lace curtains. The satin sofa had been by the fireplace and she had sat on it, beside the mother who held her hand so kindly as they listened to little blond Lucrece playing the piano.

Now there was no mother there, no Nora or Lizzie. Nobody was ringing a tinkling bell and nobody was answering. It was all so sad and so lonely. She would never, never, never—no positively never—ever come back here again.

The Leaper was nowhere to be seen as she crossed the garden.

THE SEVEN SLINKY SISTERS

Maureen was getting herself out of the gate when the scream of police sirens split the air and a car ground to a stop at the curb just outside. The police! They would arrest her!

"In here," called a familiar little voice. The Leaper was leaping off the wall and diving into a clump of bushes. He motioned her to follow. "Quick! It's the cops."

She followed him into the bushes, just in time, as a captain followed by three police officers ripped aside the boards easily, climbed inside, and ran over the garden.

"Lie low," the Leaper whispered, "and not a sound out of yez."

The policemen ran in and out of the summerhouse, beat the bushes at the back of the garden, turned flash-lights into the shadowy corners of the wall behind the trees. Once, a flashlight played up and down over the Leaper as he sat cross-legged in the bushes. They thought he was a garden ornament, he was sitting so still. Had they moved the flashlight across, instead of up and down, they would have seen a little girl in a red sweater sitting cross-legged beside him—no ornament.

"Nobody out here, Captain," called the officers.

"Look in the house there," he ordered. "There's some kind of a light there."

The Leaper and Maureen could see Ingrid standing serenely in the hallway, a candle in one hand, a pigeon sitting on each shoulder and one on top of her large velvet hat with the plume, another on the newel post, two on the third step. The Leaper leaned forward. The Pigeon Ladies had never faced the officers before. Something was up.

The police captain bustled up to her. "What's the idea, lady, bustin' in here with this poultry?" He looked at the pigeons in disgust. "Take a look upstairs, boys."

The three officers didn't race up the stairs. They moved slowly, looking back down at Ingrid with the pigeons sitting so still around her and on her.

"Who are you," the captain demanded, "and what are you doing in here?"

Ingrid raised her head haughtily. "Please," she rebuked him, "remember your manners when you are speaking to your betters. I am Ingrid Messerman."

"Well, well, well." The captain removed his hat. "Say, I beg your pardon."

He called up the stairs, "It's all right, boys. It's in the family."

"Excuse me, Miss Messerman," he went on, and there was a sheepish smile on his face. "We're looking for a crowd of shoplifters supposed to be located here— the Seven Slinky Sisters."

"Shoplifters?" Ingrid looked so innocent. "What on earth is that?"

"Say." The captain was frowning. "Didn't I hear when I was a little boy that the Messerman sisters had gone away a long long time ago?"

"We flew back," she answered sweetly, "on a whim."

"On a what?" he asked. "Is that a new kind of airplane?"

Ingrid didn't answer that. "We were living in a lovely old mansion in southern Indiana, with Victorian cupolas and wrought-iron trim."

"Sounds nice," said the captain.

"Except," she continued grandly, "when we lived in a ten-story, castle-type home on the shore of a large lake."

"It must be nice to be rich." He was studying her.

"Although," she went on, "we were also quite fond of our chateau in the midst of a Japanese garden by the side of a rushing river. But for some years now, we have been here."

"That so?" The captain's voice was respectful, but he

119

kept looking around the empty house and at the dusty floors, suspiciously.

"You ever see any stolen goods hidden away in here?" he asked.

Ingrid apparently did not like this question. "Kindly remember to whom you are speaking, and thank you so much for dropping in, you and your men upstairs."

The captain didn't seem to take the hint or know that he was being dismissed. He was still very curious about it all.

"These birds you got here?" he asked, studying the pigeons on the stairs, "and the ones you're wearing? Pets, I suppose."

"Pets?" she smiled. "Oh, no. Relatives. Please hold this." She handed him her candle. Then, with her eyes on his all the while, she began to raise and lower her arms, as though a gym teacher were calling, "And-a-one, and-a-two, and-a-three—"

She went faster and faster, all the while smiling sweetly into his staring eyes. There was a sizz-sizz-sizzling sound, a popping noise. As Maureen gasped and the officer staggered back a step, Ingrid disappeared. In her place stood a large bird, the size of a turkey, flapping its wings and shrinking with each flap until now a gray pigeon waddled across the hall into the drawing room, followed by six others.

"So that's how they do it," the Leaper muttered. "They're a disgrace to all decent pigeons."

They could see, sitting out in the bushes, how the captain grabbed hold of the stairpost to steady himself. From the flame of the candle, still grasped tightly in his hand, they could see his open mouth and his glassy, terrified eyes. He was every inch a police officer, and he crossed the hall after the pigeons into the drawing room.

They could hear him bawling out loudly, "Come back here, you birds. You're under arrest."

Then they heard a loud crashing sound like a chandelier falling. The officers raced down the stairs, their flashlights stabbing the darkening hallway. One officer held the door open as two more helped the injured captain across the garden to the gate. The Leaper and Maureen could hear them asking, "You all right, Captain?"

They saw him nod and then mutter, "Arrest those pigeons."

"Sure," they told him, "sure, sure. You lie down awhile and you'll feel lots better." They were humoring him.

The sirens screamed down the street. Seven pigeons were strutting proudly on the roof. Then they huddled close together, looking down at Maureen with beady black eyes.

They were watching her so intently they didn't see the little figure on the roof stealing up behind them. Maureen had been watching them so horrified that she didn't know when the Leaper had left her side and swung himself from the top of a tree onto the roof. He had something in his hand. It was a net, probably part of an old tennis net he had found in the summerhouse, or maybe a large fishnet. He had it over the pigeons so quickly and tied it so fast!

How they fluttered and flapped as he waved the sack back and forth.

Then he leaped to a tree, slid down, and jumped through the air to the pool with the iron boy.

"They could do with a long, long drink," he told Maureen, his eyes twinkling. And he swung the sack full of birds around and around and around in circles so as to make it fall with a hard splash into the water. "They're bad birds, and they always was."

Maureen didn't know a minute before that she would run to him, crying out, "No. No. Don't. Please, please, no."

"No?" He stopped swinging. "No? And why not? They're demons and cause lots of trouble."

But he walked close to her, dragging the sack behind him, looking up into her face as the birds fluttered frantically, crazily in the net.

"I asked yez—why not?"

"I dreamed," she told him, "there was a woman— their mother—and she came into my room up there." She pointed to the third floor of the old mansion. "And she said if I ever could, to please help them."

The birds stopped fluttering and lay quietly in the net, not making a sound.

The Leaper looked across the garden and his eyes were like seawater again, as they were the first day she'd come there and he'd talked about the lady. He untied the top of the sack slowly. The birds flew up over the trees, into the sky, until they became tiny specks in the air, and then nothing at all.

"Where will they go?" she asked.

"Who knows?" He stroked his beard. "Some fine old house somewhere. That's all they care for—finery. But wherever they go, her love will follow—from tomorrow to yesterday and back to today."

Then he told her the story of the house and the people who'd lived in it, of the day the seven sisters had gone away, of the night they'd come back and found everyone gone.

"Didn't they even cry—one tear?" she asked after a while.

"Nary a one." He shook his head. "The only sad sigh was over some clothes. They were birdbrains and

so they turned themselves into birds. Nobody ever stands still."

"I'd cry," she said after a bit, "if I came home and there was nobody there."

Then she jumped up. "Home! I've got to go home!" And she ran across the garden.

"Goodbye to yez," he called after her, "and good luck."

"Goodbye to you, too." She didn't stop running. "And good luck to you, too."

Then she was gone.

"Well, well," said he to himself, "and I always said, didn't I, that some good might come of it sometime?"

He saw now a black thing, sitting on the top of a back chimney. The cat, he told himself as he looked up at the shape with two sharp pointed ears silhouetted against the pinkish evening sky.

"How did that cat get up there?" he wondered, and, as he was wondering, he saw the thing raise wings out wide like a man in an evening cloak raising both arms hailing a taxi. He saw it glide, softly and beautifully, off the chimney top and across the garden.

It was the owl, the horned owl with a wingspread of four feet. The Leaper had seen him in the Old Messerman Place once or twice before. And he always meant bad news. While he was pondering what that could be, he heard two men talking as they went down the walk.

"They're tearing this old place down next week and black-topping it for a parking lot." Now he knew what the horned owl had come to tell him, and why Ingrid had been so bold with the captain. Tearing it down! Soon the Old Messerman Place would be gone, and nobody would ever remember what had been there any more than you remember what was written in chalk on a blackboard before the eraser rubbed it out.

"Oh, well," he told himself, "things change." And he was never surprised at change. Where would he go now? He didn't worry. He would go someplace.

Then he decided to listen back. He could do this easily. So he listened to the piano playing an old song as the young people were grouped around it a long time ago.

Wait 'til the sun shines, Nellie, and the clouds go rolling by. We will be happy, Nellie, you and I.

His projection was good, but his voice bad. Somebody was sure to call the police.

When Maureen came to the kitchen door, she didn't open it partway and thrust one arm inside. She opened the door and walked in. Her mother was standing at the kitchen sink. As she turned around, Maureen saw, for the first time, that there was gray in her hair. And in her eyes, as she saw Maureen, there was the same anxious look she had seen in the eyes of the Messerman mother.

"Where have you been?" Her voice was cross.

Even though the television was blaring upstairs, Henry, Diane, and Mr. Swanson heard her and came into the kitchen. They all frowned at Maureen. She didn't mind at all. They didn't look through her or past her.

"Answer me," Mrs. Swanson demanded. "I asked you, where have you been?"

"I've been at the Old Messerman Place."

There was silence in the kitchen.

"Didn't we tell you, never, never go there?" Mr. Swanson asked her quietly. But his tone was deadly. "So why did you do it?"

She heard herself saying, "I went to take back that bracelet."

Henry cried out, "Mother! She told the truth. Maureen told the truth."

Diane said, "I knew she took that bracelet."

Mr. Swanson said, "She said she did, in a straightforward manner, for once."

"Like a little lady." Mrs. Swanson was so happy. "Like a truthful, perfect little lady."

*   *   *

That night at dinner, when Mrs. Swanson remarked, "You're not eating, Maureen," she didn't answer, "Not eating Maureen! How could I eat myself?"

She asked a question. "Did you call me?"

"Call you?" Her mother frowned. "When?"

"When I was late today—home from school?"

"Call you?" Mr. Swanson laughed. "She yelled herself hoarse, all up and down the walk outside the Old Messerman Place."

"Did you hear me?" Her mother was watching her face.

Maureen nodded. "I heard you." But she didn't say anything more—then or ever.

MARY CHASE decided to become a writer at age seven and never wavered from that goal. She spent fourteen years as a reporter for the *Rocky Mountain News* in Denver, Colorado, then turned her attention to plays and novels. Her best-known play, *Harvey*, ran for more than four years on Broadway and was awarded the Pulitzer Prize for Drama. This play was later made into the now-classic movie starring Jimmy Stewart.

Ms. Chase was inducted into the Colorado Women's Hall of Fame and the Colorado Performing Arts Hall of Fame following her death in 1981.

PETER SÍS studied painting and filmmaking at the Academy of Applied Arts in Prague and at the Royal College of Art in London. He has written and illustrated many award-winning books for children, among them *Starry Messenger* and *Tibet: Through the Red Box*, which were both distinguished as Caldecott Honor Books. Peter Sís lives with his wife, Terry Lajtha, and their two children in New York.